Dancing with Deception

THE MORGAN BROTHERS BOOK 2

BY AVERY GALE

© Copyright 2016 by Avery Gale
ISBN 978-1-944472-29-0
All cover art and logo © Copyright 2016 by Avery Gale
All rights reserved.

The Morgan Brothers® and Avery Gale® are registered trademarks

Cover Design by Jess Buffett
Published by Avery Gale Books

Thank you for respecting the hard work of this author.

This is a work of fiction. Names, places, characters and incidents either are the product of the author's imagination or are used fictitiously and any resemblance to any actual persons, living or dead, organizations, events or locales are entirely coincidental.

No part of this book may be reproduced, stored in a retrieval system, or transmitted by any means without the written permission of the author and publishing company.

WARNING: The unauthorized reproduction or distribution of this copyrighted work is illegal. Criminal copyright infringement, including infringement without monetary gain, is investigated by the FBI and is punishable by up to 5 years in federal prison and a fine of $250,000.

If you find any books being sold or shared illegally, please contact the author at avery.gale@ymail.com.

Chapter One

"DANCE WITH ME, minx." Brandt knew he'd surprised Joelle when he shackled her slender wrist with his hand. He'd deliberately used the more aggressive move rather than simply taking her hand in his, preferring the unspoken message that he wasn't going to take no for an answer. Giving the elusive imp the opportunity to refuse would have been foolish. And for once, fate worked in his favor, when he spun her into his arms, the music slowed giving him the perfect excuse to pull her flush against his chest. Tucking her close, Brandt led her around the dance floor in a slow two-step. Keeping her tight against him sent an inordinate amount of blood racing to his cock leaving her little doubt about the effect she had on him. *Damn thing wants to do an entirely different kind of dance.*

He waited until they'd been dancing several minutes before he spoke against her ear, "You've been avoiding me." He hadn't phrased it as a question because he didn't need to ask. She'd stayed a step ahead of him all evening, but they both knew she'd only been successful because he'd allowed it. For the first part of the evening, he'd enjoyed the chase. But as the festivities proceeded, his amusement turned to frustration.

"Yes, I have." He knew she'd intended for the clipped answer to fend off the "Come to Jesus" conversation she sensed coming her way, but Brandt hadn't missed the slight quiver in her voice. The tiny verbal stumble cracked open the door of her vulnerability and he intended to storm though it in typical Navy SEAL fashion. Some lessons, once learned, weren't easy to forget; it didn't matter he'd retired from the teams, the "take no prisoners" point of view would always be a large part of who he was.

"Why?" Brandt didn't have any intention of letting her control the conversation with terse answers. The alpha male part of him was never far below the surface, and everything about her cryptic response brought the sexual Dominant inside him surging forward—finally. Hell, Brandt had worried what had once been a large part of his personality had been suppressed forever. Damn, it was a relief to feel the familiar surge of power moving through his veins again.

He'd only visited his favorite club once since he'd moved back to Pine Creek. It wasn't that he didn't enjoy spending time with the like-minded members of Mountain Mastery. Hell, Nathaniel Ledek, the owner of the club, had been a member of his SEAL team until retiring two years before Brandt had finally walked away. Ledek, who'd quickly earned the nickname "Mr. Big" for an obvious reason, had quickly parlayed his interest in kink into some serious cash by opening his own club.

Big had called him several times over the past year, asking him to act as a dungeon monitor, suggesting subs Brandt would enjoy playing with, and in general pushing and prodding at every opportunity. But Brandt hadn't gotten his feet under him enough to play yet. And he'd realized if he didn't even have control over himself, he damned well wouldn't top a woman who'd trusted him enough to gift him with her submission.

Brandt's last few missions before retiring had stolen far

too much of his humanity. And, he was self-aware enough to know there was a very real chance he wouldn't have the control necessary to play safely—which meant he wouldn't play at all. Brandt had gone to the club once with Phoenix but spent the entire evening sitting at the bar talking to Big. His friend had understood why he was taking his time getting back into the lifestyle that had been such a big part of his sexual identity, and Big had made a point of encouraging Brandt to visit anytime he needed to talk. There were so many horrific memories of his last eighteen months as a SEAL, and frankly most people couldn't possibly understand what it was like to be exposed to the darkest side of mankind. But Big had *known*.

Joelle stiffened against him at the question, whatever her reason was for avoiding him it obviously wasn't something she was particularly anxious to share. Pressing a soft kiss against the sensitive skin behind her ear, he hummed, "Don't lie to me, minx—I'll know, and then we'll have another issue to deal with as well."

Several seconds passed before she finally spoke. "You're dangerous. And I don't think I'm the kind of woman you'd be interested in." He couldn't really argue with her first statement, but he would damned well dispute the second.

"Just for the sake of clarification, you don't think I'm dangerous to you personally, do you?" Brandt tried to cover his concern with amusement, but he wasn't sure he'd been successful when she pulled back enough to look up into his eyes.

"Yes...but probably not in the way you're thinking." They'd danced their way to the back of the room close to the darkened hallway leading to the rear entrance of the pool area. This time, he clasped her small hand in his much larger one and led her through the dark. "Where are we going?"

"I want to talk to you and I don't want an audience. And in case you hadn't noticed, we were attracting a lot of attention—it's one of the hazards of having a large family. *And a job where everybody thinks you are public property and they're privy to your personal life because you are an elected official.*

JOELLE'S ENTIRE BODY was vibrating with sexual awareness, damn, there was something about Brandt Morgan that set her on fire. She'd enjoyed feeling all those rock hard muscles pressed against her and prayed he wouldn't notice how her body responded to his touch. She'd tried to distract him by complimenting his remarkable dancing skills, but he'd laughed away the compliment. "Mama Morgan made certain we all learned. She insisted she wanted to be able to dance with us at our weddings someday, and she didn't want us stepping on her feet. I suspect her real motives were somewhat different, but she knew we'd never want to hurt her, so the arguments were few and far between."

Joelle had almost panicked when he started down the dim hall. She'd never been particularly fond of the dark. Her discomfort was probably a consequence of being left alone in her bedroom by the nannies her father had hired when she was a child. But whatever the cause, it was a fear she'd brought into adulthood. He must have sensed her unease because he'd stopped just outside a door. She felt him studying her even though she could barely make out his features in the dim light. She sensed rather than saw him leaning close and thought for a second he was going to kiss her, but he'd pressed the side of his cheek against hers so his words wafted softly over the shell of her ear, "Do you trust me, minx?"

Trust him? Was he kidding? Right now he was rocketing to the top of her "Most Dangerous People on the Planet" list. Joelle wasn't a fool, she knew an Alpha Male when she met one, and Brandt Morgan was as Alpha as they came. Pulling in a deep breath, ready to tell him no, knowing it would be enough to make him pull back. But evidently all those "I want to fuck him until neither of us can walk" hormones had taken her common sense hostage because she felt herself nod before her brain kicked fully into gear. "Not good enough, minx. Say it out loud. It'll help cement it in your mind even if you aren't as convinced as you want me to think you are."

Drown him. How had he known when it was darker than the inside of a freaking cat in this damned hallway? It's not like he could actually see her, but he'd somehow sensed her reticence. Deciding it was easier to answer the question than to puzzle it out, she breathed out the words, enjoying the rasp of his five o'clock shadow against her cheek. "Yes, I trust you. I don't believe you'd hurt me." *At least not physically.* She left the last part unsaid but wondered if he'd heard it in her voice anyway.

"Close enough. Come." She heard him tap in a code on a keypad she hadn't noticed. Stepping through the door, Joelle noted they'd stepped into what looked like a locker room. He didn't say anything, just tugged her along as he weaved a path through the lockers and benches. She caught the scent of chlorine a few seconds before they stepped into the pool area she'd barely noticed from the other side of the large glass wall.

"Wow, this is spectacular." Joelle didn't even try to censor her response because the Morgan's pool was absolutely stunning. Having grown up privileged, she was no stranger to beautiful spaces, but this was breathtaking...and much larger than she'd expected. The lush tropical landscaping around the enormous pool provided an illusion of privacy for the various seating areas. Guests would be able to enjoy the intimacy of small groups without feeling completely isolated. Smooth flagstones lined paths wide enough for two people to walk side-by-side. They wove through the colorful foliage that reminded Joelle of the tropical resorts her father had taken her to as a child. God, she'd loved those trips, they'd been rare occasions when she'd had the majority of his attention for a few days.

But it was the enormous rock waterfall that drew her like a moth to a flame. She'd always loved the sound of falling water, it soothed everything unsettled in her heart and mind. She unconsciously changed direction, walking toward the waterfall. She didn't even realize she was tugging him along until she heard him chuckle. "What is it about that damned waterfall? My mom and Coral are both as enthralled by it as you are, minx."

"Moving water...particularly falling water and waves, positively charges the ions in the air. It gives people relief from the negativity so often surrounding them, sort of a "feel good boost" compliments of Mother Nature." *Damn. Nothing like sounding like a science nerd.*

BRANDT STRUGGLED TO hold back his laughter—damn, Phoenix had definitely nailed this one. There was a lot more to Joelle than what she wanted anyone to see. One thing Brandt learned a long time ago—it's as hard to hide intelligence as it is to hide ignorance over a long period of time. Not wanting to tip his hand, he simply nodded before turning her so she was facing away from the waterfall. She'd still be able to hear it, but he wanted her eyes on him. He didn't say anything, he simply watched her for long seconds. When she started to fidget under his scrutiny, he used his fingers under her chin to bring her focus back to him. "Eyes on me, minx." Watching her pupils dilate with arousal at his command confirmed what he already suspected—there was a submissive buried deep inside the feisty redhead.

"Now, I want you to tell me what you meant by your earlier comment. What makes you believe I wouldn't be interested in you?" *Because, baby, I'm telling you now—I've more than a little interested already.* Letting out an exasperated sigh, she rolled her eyes bringing the sexual Dominant in him roaring to the surface. Before he could rein it in, he growled, "Be very careful, minx. Those little signs of disrespect won't serve you well."

Her eyes widened for a split second in recognition and Brandt wanted to smile when she immediately dropped her gaze to the floor. *Oh yes indeed, there is definitely a sub in there, and one who appears to have at least a subconscious awareness of the fact she's a sub. Jesus, Joseph, and Mary, has she been trained?* That question flooded him with a white hot flash of jealousy so intense it shocked him. Hell, he'd never felt anything close to possessive of a submissive before.

"Well, I just meant that I'm just a clerk in a small town drug store." Brandt wasn't going to listen to her blow smoke up his ass, particularly when it was glaringly apparent her story was bogus. Even a passing understanding of Dominance and submission would have taught her that lying in any form was unacceptable—so she fucking knew better than to try it.

"Stop. Don't insult my intelligence with drivel." He watched her lips firm in a stubborn line that would get her a paddling she wouldn't soon forget if she belonged to him. He opened his mouth to tell her to try again when he heard someone pounding on the glass behind him. Turning, he saw his mother motioning for them to come out. She was talking a mile a minute even though she had to know they couldn't hear her, and the only word he'd been able to make out was "bouquet."

Brandt nodded once at his mother before leading Joelle toward the door. Looking down at her, he wanted to snarl his frustration. "Don't look so smug, minx. You've gotten a temporary reprieve, but I assure you, this conversation is far from over." Seeing the grin on Joelle's face when he handed her over to his mother made his palm twitch in anticipation. *You'd look lovely with your bare ass draped over my lap, minx.* He barely managed to keep the comment to himself as her fingers slipped from his.

Moving to one of the large tubs set-up in front of the bar, Brandt pulled a bottle of water from the ice and downed the contents in a few gulps. Kip bent close to be heard over the music. "Mom can have really lousy timing sometimes." The youngest Morgan brother was leaning with his back against the bar grinning like a fucking loon. Kip was fun loving and considering his reputation with the ladies, Brandt didn't doubt his little brother had given their mom numerous opportunities to interrupt his amorous adventures.

Nodding, Brandt agreed, "That she does, but my conversation with Ms. Freemont is far from finished. She made a comment about not being the type of woman I'd be interested in." Kip didn't respond, but his brow arched up letting Brandt know he also recognized the comment as a lame excuse at the very least. Personally, Brandt was more inclined to see it as a blatant lie. "And then she had the audacity to try to blow smoke up my ass by playing the *I'm just a lowly drug store clerk card.*" This time, Kip laughed out loud.

"Hope you called bull shit because she's sharp as a tack. And Barney swears she knows more about most of the drugs in his inventory than he does. She's also implemented new security protocols. The old fart told me he was shocked at the difference in his profit margin—seems more than a few of the store's narcotics were walking out the door in his employee's pockets." Barney Knapp was Pine Creek's only pharmacist. Brandt knew the elderly man wanted to retire, but he'd put off moving to a warmer climate because he didn't want to leave his hometown without a pharmacy. Brandt appreciated the man's loyalty to the community but wasn't at all pleased this was the first he'd heard about the drug thefts.

"God damn it, why didn't I know about this?"

The knowing look in Kip's eyes made Brandt want to slap his kid brother upside the head. "Wow, lemme' think. Don't suppose it's *this* reaction, do you?" *Fuck!* Had he really been such an ass the citizens he'd sworn to protect were afraid to talk to him? "Aww…I see a spark of awareness flickering to life. And the answer to the question I see in your eyes is *yes*, you've been a douche in varying degrees since you moved home. But we love you and we're trying to be patient—but it's probably time to yank your head out of your ass before the scales tip in the other direction."

Running his hand through his short hair in frustration,

Brandt could only nod. It was true—he wasn't the easy-going kid who'd left Pine Creek more than a decade ago. That young man had slowly faded from existence during his years as a SEAL. Having a front row seat to the brutality and senseless loss of life—which were always a part of war, had a way of eroding even the strongest among them and wasn't it just happy-fucking-humbling having your kid brother point it out to you?

"Just because I'm a nosy little bastard I'm going to ask—you aren't going to let the little sub get away with that nonsense are ya? Because I gotta tell ya, I can see her topping from the bottom every chance she gets."

Brandt shook his head. "First off, you are indeed a nosy bastard, but apparently observant as well. Hell, how did you know she was submissive? I wasn't absolutely sure until a few minutes ago though I had my suspicions. And I'm sure I've spent more time with her than you have."

"Well, you've been courting her—even if neither of you knew it. But me? Like I said, I'm just nosy so I have more time to observe, and one of the things I noticed is how you failed to answer my question." With that, Kip tipped his bottle of beer in Brandt's direction, pushed away from the wall, and headed back into the crowd.

"Hey, kid brother." When Kip turned, Brandt grinned. "Thanks for the kick in the pants, and fuck no I'm not going to ignore it. Maybe I'll head down to Billings this weekend and hit the club. A chat with Nathanial might be in order." Kip grinned, giving him a mock salute. Yeah, a long conversation with his friend and mentor at Mountain Mastery would go a long way to help him sort this out.

Phoenix grabbed another beer and leaned against the bar. He watched his older brother dancing with Joelle wondering if she would finally tell him about her security concerns. Hell, Phoenix would be happy if the pretty redhead would tell Brandt who she really was. Admittedly the name she was using was real, even if it was misleading simply because it was incomplete. Not using your surname wasn't exactly making your best effort to hide, but since he didn't understand why she was laying low, he wasn't going to judge.

When Joelle contacted him to design and install a state of the art security system in her small house at the edge of town, Phoenix had been stunned at the scale of protection she'd requested. He'd questioned her simply because it seemed like a significant level of overkill for Pine Creek. It had taken him hours of heartfelt promises to keep her confidence before he'd finally convinced her to confide in him. He hadn't told her how easily he could have run her through his facial recognition software—it would have given him her real name within a matter of hours. Knowing she'd finally put her trust in him had been far more satisfying than snooping into her personal information—of course once he'd known her real name, he started wondering why she was living in Pine Creek. There was a lot of internet chatter and speculation, but nobody seemed to know for sure why she'd vanished.

Joelle Freemont Phillips was not only a billionaire heiress, but she was also a brilliant researcher and chemist. Her work within her father's pharmaceutical division was well respected. None of the internet gossip he'd read mentioned what she'd been working on when she disappeared, but since her father hadn't contacted authorities, everyone assumed he knew where she was.

The more he'd read, the stranger the entire situation seemed, and oddly enough—out of all the unknowns, the one thing that struck him as particularly odd was the lack of information about her social life. As the member of a wealthy family, Phoenix understood the need for discretion in his personal life, but even a casual search on-line for his brothers turned up speculation about their sexual predilection even if their interests in kink hadn't been confirmed. But the complete lack of information about Joelle meant she was either a saint or incredibly discreet.

All the components for her upgraded security system were ready to install and he hoped to get things set up for her sooner rather than later, because anytime there was a lack of information on-line, the hair on the back of his neck stood up. He'd promised to keep their business arrangement private and Phoenix didn't want to betray her confidence—at least not until he had no other choice.

Chapter Two

BRANDT LEANED CASUALLY against the wall near the club's bar and tipped the bottle of water to his lips. He wasn't planning to play tonight, but he doubted Phoenix would be in any condition to drive home since he was making his way up the spiral staircase heading to a private party with one of the club's submissives. Phoenix wasn't known for partying, but when he did let go, Brandt knew his younger brother could drink the rest of the Morgan brothers under the table. Phoenix wouldn't drink until after their scene, but he'd certainly hit the bar later. The combination of fatigue and alcohol meant Brandt would be driving them home.

"Looks like Phoenix's found himself a sub for the evening. Hope he ate his Wheaties; Kitty is a handful." Mountain Mastery's owner grinned. When Brandt looked at his friend in question, he shook his head. "Don't get me wrong, Kitty is a sweet girl, but she pushes Doms to their limit. I've seen her send experienced Doms into orbit with her antics. The last time one of the Dungeon Monitors had to intercede I paddled her myself. I'm sure she didn't sit comfortably for days. But I doubt it made a lasting impression."

"Perhaps it did since she's going to play in a private room tonight?" Brandt had to suppress his laughter when his friend groaned. "Don't worry, Phoenix is remarkably insightful when it comes to women—she'll play hell getting around him."

"Glad to hear it. To be honest, she is one of two subs I've been wondering what to do with. I've been worried we aren't meeting either of the women's needs." Brandt could hear the concern in Big's voice and wondered what the issue was with the second woman. He saw the other man's eyes move to a nearby scene, whatever the club's owner saw didn't set well because he frowned and pushed away from the wall. "Come on. I'd be interested to hear your opinion on this one."

Making their way through the small audience gathered around the St. Andrews cross, Big leaned close, "JoJo has come in a couple times a month for the last six or seven months. She never scenes with the same Dom twice and she never lets them fuck her." Brandt finally stepped around the man who'd been blocking his view and sucked in a breath. *No fucking way.* It couldn't be her. He heard himself growl and Big turned in his direction. "Do you know her?"

Brandt's jaw was going to shatter he was clenching his teeth so hard. He'd been trying to catch up with Joelle all week, but she'd stonewalled him at every turn. When he'd finally cornered her in the drug store yesterday, she'd told him she already had plans this evening. No fucking shit, she had plans. Plans to let another man touch what— somewhere in the back of his mind, Brandt already considered his. Plans to let another man get her off—give her the sexual release Brandt longed to provide. *Fucking hell.*

Big shook his head, "Christ, she's the one you were talking about isn't she?" They'd had a long discussion upstairs in Big's office before the club opened. As Brandt's mentor and a former member of the teams, Big was in a unique position to understand what Brandt had been going through since returning home. The club owner understood Brandt's concern the darkness in him could overtake his control. But Big insisted—in most cases the trauma they'd experienced actually amplified previously existing personality traits. Since Brandt's ability to control his emotions had been almost legendary among Special Forces members, Big assured him there was little chance his personality had done a complete one-eighty. When Brandt nodded in response to Big's inquiry, he heard a string of creative cursing the former SEAL was well known for. *Not helping, Big. Not helping at all.*

"Listen, I don't know her story, but I've suspected from the beginning her application is missing a lot of very important details. Our investigation didn't turn up any lies, but her background is squeaky clean." *Yeah and we all know anything too good to be true usually is too good to be true.*

"Phoenix and I have made that same observation. And she's much more educated than she wants anyone to know—not something easily concealed over any length of time."

"Agreed. I think it's probably easier to hide ignorance if you want to know the truth. Hell, we've both seen military leaders who made their way up the ranks because they were masters of baffling with bull shit." They continued watching what Brant was certain was the worst scene between a Dom and a sub he'd ever watched.

"Now, let's get back to the fact I don't think this little sub is getting what she needs." As they stood shoulder to shoulder watching for the next few minutes, Brandt agreed, the damned scene was almost painful to watch and it certainly wasn't going anywhere. "You up for a challenge, brother? Because I'm getting the vibe you aren't overly thrilled with the fact Master Raef has his hands on your woman." *His woman?* Was he ready to acknowledge how possessive he felt about Joelle? Shaking his head, Brandt only knew one thing for certain—fate had taken away his ability to pussyfoot around making a decision. She'd put him squarely on Front Street—it was time to put up or shut up.

"Yes. But tell me, how often does she fake her responses?"

Big looked at him and grinned. "Didn't figure you would miss that, even though her top tonight seems oblivious."

"Going to send him back through training again?" Brandt knew his friend would probably counsel the young man first because sending him back through the Dom classes would be damned humiliating for the man who from what Brandt could see wasn't actually doing that bad. It was the submissive tied in front of him who was derailing the scene. But *Jo-Jo* was about to get a taste of what it was like to deal with a Dom who understood the game she was playing.

"No, he's just nervous. This is his first scene in the main lounge area, and I'd say she's had a lot of practice faking it. I'd bet there aren't ten men in the room who've noticed." Brandt shook his head finding it difficult to believe her act would fool anyone who was actually paying attention. "Since she's already blindfolded, I'm going to leave her that way, but let me get him redirected first."

Brandt nodded and moved to stand in front of Joelle while Big pulled the young Dom to the side. He couldn't hear what the club's owner said to him, but the man's expression had gone from apprehensive because he'd been called out of his scene to relieved. Brandt laughed to himself, evidently Nate's people skills had improved since he'd left the Special Forces. The young Dom returned to gather his equipment, stuffing everything in his bag, before nodding to Brandt and then leaning in to whisper something in Joelle's ear. Brandt felt his entire body tense in response—something deep inside him was screaming *"Mine"* and for several seconds, the sound of his blood pounding in his ears drowned out everything around him.

As the other man stood back, Joelle started to tremble, shaking her head back and forth. Even with her eyes covered, Brandt sensed her sudden fear. Her entire body was beginning to shudder and he worried she was within seconds of using her safe word. It was time to head things in a different direction because that certainly wasn't how he wanted this to play out.

Stepping in front of her, he made sure he was close enough she would sense his presence. He watched her entire body tense when she became aware of the fact someone was standing close. Drawing his finger along the bottom curve of her jaw, he leaned close. "Shhh. You are fine." Brandt wanted to calm her but hadn't wanted to say enough she'd recognize his voice. Nate needed a chance to speak with her first. She'd broken one of the club's cardinal rules by faking her responses during a scene, and it was up to Big to explain the consequences of her decision before Brandt took over.

Brandt stepped aside as Big approached. "JoJo, you have gotten yourself in quite a predicament this time." She obviously recognized Master Nate's voice because the trembling returned, but this time, Brandt sensed her fear was entirely different. "Here are your choices, pet. I can release you so you can leave the club, which means you'll forfeit your membership. Or you can agree to a public scene which I'll advertise in advance. You'll spend an hour in the stocks while any Dom in attendance will be given the opportunity to administer five strokes with the implement of his choice."

Joelle's panic was now obvious, she was shaking so hard Brandt worried she was going to have bruises where her wrists and ankles were moving violently against the restraints. The movement hadn't escaped Big's attention because he wrapped his large hands around her forearms stilling her movements. "Your third option is to allow me to choose a Dom who will continue tonight's scene. You'll submit to him because you trust me to put you in the care of a man I have known for many years—a man I trust to provide you with exactly what you need." Big remained silent for several long seconds giving Joelle time to consider the options he'd given her.

Brandt was relieved when she responded quickly. "I'll continue the scene...if you're sure I'll be safe."

"I would never leave you in the care of a man I didn't trust implicitly. We both know you haven't been getting what you need here, pet. Until further notice, this man will be the only one you play with at Mountain Mastery, do you understand?"

"Yes, sir." Her voice trembled, but her response had been clear enough. Brandt hated seeing the single tear slide beneath the blindfold. He didn't mind tears under the right circumstances, but fear wasn't on that short list.

Big stepped back and directed his attention to Brandt. "I'm counting on you to take good care of her. Make sure she understands the difference between genuine arousal and what she thinks will appease her Dom."

Brandt nodded in agreement as he stepped forward. The other Dom's first mistake had been letting Joelle keep her corset and skirt on. The skirt was short enough it was easy to see she wasn't wearing panties, but she still had the illusion of being covered—and that false sense of security was going to end in short order.

Brandt wondered if she'd ever fully submitted to a Dom—he doubted it, but that too was about to change. Reaching forward, he began unlacing the ties of her corset. When she started shaking her head no, he stopped, giving her time to rethink her objection. She took several deep breaths and he could practically hear her mind running back through the options Nate had given.

"I'm...I'm sorry. I just don't like being naked in front of strangers." He didn't respond, but he did wait until she settled to continue. "Sir?" When he didn't respond, she tensed. Brandt knew what was coming and he welcomed the challenge. He would make the most of her defiance—hell, maybe it would keep him focused long enough to finish the scene without embarrassing himself like an inexperienced teenager. "Sir? Did you hear me?" He stepped back letting her feel the disconnection. Moving to the side, he gave her ass two solid swats. She gasped in surprise but didn't comment. *Smart girl.*

The submissive part of Joelle's personality wasn't easy to detect outside of the club, but here they both knew the rules. There had been a spark of rebellion in her tone that made Brandt half crazed with desire. He'd never been attracted to women who were so totally submissive they lost themselves in their Dom. Where was the fun in having a woman gift you with her trust if she was nothing but a robot? Mindless submission didn't appeal to him at all. "I'm sorry, sir." The words were airy, and despite the fact they'd been filled with apprehension he knew things were turning around because he could smell her arousal.

Leaning close, Brandt used the very tips of his fingers to move her hair over her shoulder, baring the side of her neck to his touch. Pressing his lips against her pounding pulse, he nipped the lobe of her ear. "You've gotten yourself in a hell of a fix, minx." He'd known using his pet name for her would give away his identity, and he was right. What he hadn't been sure of was how she would react. Would she be embarrassed because he'd not only found out she was attending a kink club, but he'd also been put in charge of her after a disastrous scene? Or would she rebel? After all, she had been going to great lengths to avoid him all week.

He made no effort to hold back his chuckle when she sucked in a breath. Her cheeks beneath the silk scarf covering her pretty gray eyes flamed bright red and he barely heard her whispered, "Oh shit." Probably going with embarrassed and well aware that all the rules governing their common interest had just changed. Because it didn't matter what pretty little lie she was telling herself—their mutual attraction was undeniable.

Running the tip of his tongue along the outer edge of her ear, he spoke so only she could hear, "Oh shit, indeed. Minx, what were you thinking? Even a novice sub knows better than to fake a response during a scene. And I'm nobody's fool, princess. I know you are not a novice, and that's another item on the long list of things we need to discuss." He didn't really have a right to be upset she'd declined his dinner invitation to be here, but it didn't mean he was happy about it either.

"Now, since I'm a big believer in making the punishment fit the crime, I'm going to do things a bit differently tonight. I'm going to step away from you for a few seconds. You don't need to see what I'm setting up just yet so

I'm leaving the scarf in place for now. I don't want you to think I've walked away from you while you are bound, so I'm going to keep one hand on you at all times. I'll also be using the headphones to keep you from hearing the instructions I'm giving the Dungeon Monitors." He slid his hand from the side of her neck down until her breast was cradled in the palm of his hand and used the pad of his thumb to lightly abrade her pretty pink nipple. The nub pebbled even tighter and Brandt smiled at her responsiveness. "Do you understand, minx?"

There was only the briefest hesitation before she answered, letting him know she did indeed understand what he'd said. He signaled a nearby attendant, requesting headphones he'd connect to his phone rather than the club's sound system. Brandt was going to use a very specific playlist for Joelle. He planned to spin her up pretty high, so he wanted her as relaxed as possible before they started. He'd checked the volume before sliding the headphones over her ears and ran a soothing hand over her shoulder when he felt surprise move through her. He wasn't sure what she'd been expecting, but obviously, Brian Crain's soothing piano music had been a surprise.

Within minutes, the attendants and dungeon monitors had the equipment moved into place. Joelle was going to face one of her fears tonight or she'd be forced to forfeit her membership—which one would she choose?

JOELLE'S ENTIRE BODY was alight with such anticipation she was struggling to maintain even a hint of control. The soothing music playing in her ears was helping, but Brandt's touch was leaving a trail of fire sizzling over every inch he touched.

She'd been terrified when Master Nate interrupted the scene. Damn, she'd known she should have told the Dom topping her the scene wasn't working, but he'd seemed so eager she hadn't wanted to hurt his feelings. And now, he was probably pissed she'd humiliated him. She also managed to get herself in trouble with the club's owner—so not what she'd planned for this trip. And the kicker was the very man she'd been hoping to exorcise from her mind was the one Master Nathaniel put in charge of her punishment. Karma really could be a cruel bitch at times.

She'd been both relieved and terrified when she realized Brandt Morgan was the Dom who would be finishing the scene. Damn, who would have guessed he'd be a member of Mountain Mastery? *Some researcher I turned out to be.*

One of her favorite parts of BDSM was the fact that inside a club everyone was equal. Joelle had always hated that people often told her what they thought she wanted to hear rather than the truth simply because her family had money. It was a social phenomenon that had always baffled her. It was also one of the reasons she was grateful her parents had followed moneyed tradition by using her mother's maiden name as her middle name. It had been easy to drop her last name affording her a small taste of anonymity. Being able to have even a small measure of freedom from the Phillips name made her feel like a bird whose small gilded cage had been opened in a room-sized atrium. Her flight was still limited, but the illusion of freedom was there.

But at the end of the day, being honest with herself had always been the best way to stay grounded. Deep down, she'd known Brandt Morgan was an alpha male, and if she was going to be brutally honest...yes, she'd suspected he was a Dom. But suspecting and being blindsided with the information after being put in his care during an interrupted scene were two very different situations.

She let herself get lost in thought as she listened to the soulful melodies of Brian Crain. Joelle had gasped in surprise when Brandt slid the headphones over her ears and the unmistakable strains of Brian's beautiful piano music filled her ears. She'd been a fan of his for several years and she'd even met him after a performance early in his career. Realizing she and Brandt both enjoyed the same music was a strange sort of validation for her...it gave her just enough of a feeling of connection to settle her nerves as she waited for him to set up whatever he was planning. He'd kept his promise, by keeping one hand on her at all times. The small connection his touch provided kept her mind centered enough she'd been able to begin reevaluating the choices she'd made since fleeing her father's estate months ago.

The breakthrough she'd made should be making headlines, giving cancer patients all over the world the hope they deserved. But instead, it was hidden...waiting for her to be brave enough to fight back against the Board of Directors of Phillips Pharmaceutical.

Her father was still the CEO and he'd seemed enthused about her discovery. But he'd been quickly outvoted when she'd presented a synopsis of her findings to the board's members. Of course, several of those members were major stockholders in the large biomedical companies making billions of dollars every year selling medications and equipment far less effective, and in some cases little more than placebos. Two members were also major stockholders in hospitals specializing in the treatment of various forms of cancer, so their opposition had been just as adamant.

But her biggest opponent had been the board member currently running for president. If word ever got out the woman had vehemently opposed publishing the studies' results her political aspirations would be dead in the water. The voting public wouldn't take kindly to her opposition to the lifesaving treatment, and the fall-out would be devastating to her campaign. Helen Rodrick and many of her financial supporters had substantial financial interests in companies that would take a hit when Joelle's discovery came to light. Personally, Joelle considered Helen Rodrick the most dangerous of her opponents. Historically individuals having a conflict with the former senator seemed to have bizarre, often fatal accidents.

Not long after her presentation to the board, Joelle's lab was burglarized—twice, despite an elaborate security system. She'd still vowed to fight the board, submitting a formal request for reconsideration. But before the scheduled meeting, two men broke into her condo and it had been Joelle's breaking point. The intruders had been dressed from head to toe in black, including their facemasks. One held a knife to her throat as the other explained in graphic detail exactly what would happen to her and her father should she continue pushing to make the results of her research public. She'd spent the rest of the night packing, fired off a short message to her father assuring him she would be in touch, and fled.

Pine Creek hadn't been a coincidence. She'd inherited the home she was living in from an uncle she'd never met. She'd planned to sell the property, but hadn't gotten around to it—once again, fate had been one-step ahead of her. Joelle was quickly losing herself in her memories when she suddenly realized the headphones had been removed and Brandt had spoken to her, but damned if she had any clue what he'd said. She felt her face blazing with embarrassment. How had she managed to dig herself even deeper by not focusing during a scene with Brandt Morgan? Particularly a punishment scene, holy shit it was a whole new level of dim.

"Just for the record, I can practically hear your mind scrambling to remember what I asked you, minx. You'd do well to just admit you were lost in thought. But when you do, I suggest you tell me exactly where your mind was—honestly. Full disclosure is your friend, sweet sub."

Joelle took a deep breath, she really needed to confide in Brandt—not because he'd given her a command to. As the Sheriff of Pine County, he had a right to know if trouble might follow her to town and she'd already put off the conversation far longer than she should have. This wasn't the place to explain things in detail, but she owed it to him to be as transparent as she could be. She spoke quietly since she didn't know what he'd set up, so she had no idea who else might be close enough to hear. "Are you the only one who can hear me, sir?"

Chapter Three

BRANDT FROZE AT Joelle's question. He wanted her honesty, but he didn't want to do anything that would jeopardize her safety either. Since he'd already been standing in front of her, he leaned closer, letting his lips graze her ear in a move that would look like seduction to the audience but would allow her to whisper directly into his ear. "Speak softly, baby. And thank you in advance for trusting me." He wanted to encourage her and thanking her in advance was the best way he knew considering their current situation.

"I was thinking about the reason I had to run, the reason I'm still not sure I'm safe. I know I should have talked to you about it sooner, but...I didn't want you to feel."

Brandt cut her off by biting down gently on the lobe of her ear. "Shhh. We'll talk about it later...I assure you. But I want to have that conversation in private because nothing is more important than your safety." Even though her bindings gave her very little room for movement, he felt her relax against him. She pressed herself closer as some of the tension ebbed from her taut muscles and that small display of trust made his cock swell as blood abandoned his brain and headed south. *Fuck, getting through this scene without embarrassing myself is going to be a test I'm not sure I'm ready for.*

Pulling back just far enough he was able to slide his

fingers under the edges of the silk covering her eyes, he spoke loud enough for those gathered around to hear. Brandt was surprised at the size of the audience they'd drawn. But since he and his brothers rarely did public scenes, he credited the novelty of a Morgan performance with a large part of the interest. Brandt also knew Big rarely handed off punishments for this particular offense. He usually took the sub to the main stage and used one of the fucking machines to force orgasm after orgasm from the submissive. Brandt had yet to see a submissive walk away on their own from one of Big's punishments. The man was positively ruthless when it came to a submissive deliberately faking any response, particularly an orgasm. *Yeah, minx, you definitely pushed one of Big's hot buttons.*

Using the name he'd heard Big call her, Brandt spoke loud enough to quiet those whispering around them. "JoJo, tell me why you are being punished."

"I faked a release, sir." Brandt was proud of her straightforward answer, she hadn't given an excuse. She'd simply answered the question. *Good girl.*

"I'm not going to ask what you were thinking because you clearly weren't thinking." He wasn't going to force her to explain her distraction, he already suspected she hadn't been getting what she needed from the scene and had been trying to end it as soon as possible. "Since you've already admitted you aren't fond of being naked in front of strangers, it's not difficult to imagine you aren't particularly thrilled with the idea of having public orgasms." He was sure Joelle knew exactly where this was headed because her entire body was responding perfectly. Brandt was anxious to move on, he'd be able to gauge her responses much better when he could see her eyes.

"Since I'm absolutely convinced the best punishment,

in this case, is one that will force you to confront your fear of public vulnerability—that is exactly what I'm going to do." He heard her gasp as she shook her head no. Placing his hands on both sides of her face stilling her, he pressed a kiss against her forehead. Speaking softly, he asked, "Who are you supposed to please during a scene, JoJo?"

"You, sir." He wanted to fist pump at her answer. His question hadn't addressed this scene specifically, but she'd answered *very* specifically. He was thrilled somewhere deep inside, she'd already assigned him the role of her Dom. *Fucking perfect.*

"Yes, that's exactly right. Now—when I remove the blindfold, I want you to focus all of your attention on me. Your eyes should stay on mine. Do you understand?" Even though she said she did, Brandt knew the reality was going to be far more difficult. Sliding the silk off and tossing it aside, her eyes widened when they darted to his left and right. He pinched her nipples between the calloused pads of his fingers with enough force to make her hiss at the unexpected burn, Brandt hadn't wanted to cause her any unnecessary pain, but he wanted to bring her attention back to him. "Where are your eyes supposed to be, minx?"

Her soft gray eyes snapped to his, locking her gaze solidly with his. "On you, sir." The words had been airy, but not with arousal. Her soft tone was laced with something too close to fear for Brandt's taste. It was definitely time to show her this was a punishment she could enjoy if she would keep her focus on him.

Brandt slid his right hand down her torso until the tips of his fingers were poised at the very top of her slit. "Keep your eyes on me. I'm the only person in this room who matters to you right now. You've put yourself in my care and I intend to see to it both you and Master Nate are satisfied with this scene when we're finished." There was a flash of apprehension at the mention of Nate, but it didn't last long when the pad of his middle finger grazed over her clit. "Keep those pretty gray eyes focused on mine, minx. I don't want you to hide anything from me. I own each sigh, every small moan of arousal, and all those muffled gasps of pleasure."

Watching her slowly let go was one of the most erotic things Brandt had ever seen. Joelle kept her eyes focused on his until he knew they were no longer focusing on anything. As soon as he'd slid his fingers deep into her heat, fucking her with slow, steady thrusts that pressed against her G-spot with each pass, the rose blush of arousal washed over her chest. Her breathing was shallow and fast, and the steady increase in the pulse pounding at the base of her throat let him know how quickly she was approaching orgasm. *Oh, baby, you're not getting off that easy. Pun intended.*

He pulled his fingers from her and smiled when she whined in frustration. "You didn't think you were going to get to come so soon did you, minx? We've only just started to play." The truth was he'd fought damned hard to pull free of her trembling channel. Knowing she was a breath or two away from release had been the only reason he'd managed to slip his fingers from her. He'd wanted nothing more than to feel her pussy flood his hand with honey as it pulsed around his digits. Using the small remote in his pocket, Brandt engaged the hydraulics tilting the top half of wooden cross forward causing Joelle to bend forward at the waist. He knew the instant she realized how exposed she was to the audience by the way her muscles tensed. Stoking his fingers up and down the length of her spine several times, he watched as she tried to maintain her apprehension even though her body wanted to relax beneath his touch.

Drizzling lube into his palm to warm it, he met her eyes in one of the mirrors facing her. "Your eyes should stay on me, minx. No matter if I'm watching you or not, you need to remain focused on your Master. Pleasing your Dominant is your number one priority—and in this case, it means tuning out everything but me." Tucking her short skirt up in the waistband, he rimmed her exposed ass with lubed fingers. Brandt fought the urge to press his fingers deep imitating the much more intimate act he hoped to do soon in private. Her reaction to the first press of his fingers against her rear hole told him she had little to no experience with anal pleasure. Brandt wished he'd looked over her limit list before starting, but it was too late to worry about that now.

Movement to the side of the small stage caught Brandt's eye, and when he glanced over where he knew Big was standing, it was the shit-eating grin on the man standing next to him that drew his attention. His cousin Ryan stood with his feet shoulder width apart, his arms crossed over his chest. His posture was imposing, something Brandt knew from personal experience came naturally to all former Special Service members—no matter how long they'd been away from the teams. Even though they hadn't served on the same SEAL team, he and Big had worked with Ryan's team on several joint missions. The world of Special Forces was a surprisingly small and close-knit group, most of the members knew each other by reputation if not personally.

Brandt had been expecting Ryan early next week, but he wasn't surprised the younger man had shown up ahead of schedule so he could spend time at the club. He and Ryan had shared subs several times and they'd always worked well together. Brandt wondered how Joelle would react if he suggested a ménage. Damn, he really needed to get his hands on her limit list.

He felt her jerk beneath his touch and noted she'd followed his gaze. Fuck, he would have to punish her, but it really was his own fault. He didn't waste any time sliding the small plug into place. Grabbing one of the hand towels from the table behind him, Brandt wiped the lube from his fingers before tilting her further forward so there would be no doubt he'd moved her into a punishment position. Her ass was high in the air, her legs spread wide—hell there wasn't an inch of her sex that wasn't completely exposed to everyone in the audience. Kneeling in front of her, he kept the strap in his hand so there would be no doubt where things were headed. Pulling her face up to his, Brandt didn't get a chance to ask if she knew what she'd done wrong. "I'm sorry. I know I was supposed to watch you. But I was scared when you were looking to the side for so long. Is she your sub?" *What? She?*

Looking to the side, Brandt saw a petite blonde standing next to Ryan. She was clearly trying to get his cousin's attention, but Ryan didn't seem to be taking the bait. There wasn't a chance in hell Ry didn't know she was there—you don't get close to a Navy SEAL without them knowing you're there. He'd known men retired from the teams for decades who swore they still sensed people approaching long before they were close enough to do harm.

Knowing Joelle was worried he already had a submissive gave him an odd sense of satisfaction. "No, minx, she doesn't belong to me. I hadn't even planned to play this evening. But I did come here to talk to Master Nate about a woman who'd been avoiding me all week." She didn't respond, but her lips formed a perfect O letting him know she'd understood he'd been referring to her. "Oh is right. We'll have a discussion about *that* later as well, but right now I'm going to lay three stripes on your lovely ass as a reminder to follow instructions." He wasn't going to give her the ten he'd planned on—damn, he was probably making a mistake going easy on her. But he didn't want her first experience with him to be all about pain, either. Since they hadn't played together before, there wasn't any foundation of trust to rely on.

Brandt didn't give her any time to worry about what was to come, he stepped behind her and administered three solid strokes. He spaced them evenly though one lay directly over the crease between her ass and thigh—that one would be a reminder of their time together for a couple of days. He'd finished before her mind caught up. She'd hissed at the burn of the first strike, but the second and third were so quick he was finished before the heat even registered. He dropped the leather strap to the floor with a clatter and immediately pushed two fingers into her soaking wet pussy. *Yeah, I think somebody enjoys a bite of pain—fucking perfect.*

Years of being a sexual dominant gave him the experience necessary to find her G-spot in one thrust. He hadn't intended to end the scene so soon, but it was more important for her mind to link the pain and pleasure than it was to give the audience a protracted scene. Leaning close, he spoke against her ear, "Come for me, minx. I want to hear you scream your pleasure." He'd barely finished the words when he felt her vaginal walls lock down on his fingers. The rush of her honey over them made him want to shout in triumph. She screamed his name as she shattered and hearing his name cross her lips while she was in the throes of passion was incredibly satisfying. The only thing would have made the moment even sweeter—if it had been his cock rather than his fingers giving her pleasure. *Soon…very, very soon!*

JOELLE WAS SO lost in the aftershocks of the most powerful orgasm of her life, she was barely cognizant of the fact Brandt had released her from the club's strange cross. Even as she felt a soft blanket being wrapped around her, her mind and body still didn't feel like they belonged to the same person. She'd never experienced anything remotely like the disconnection she felt now—and the harder she tried to figure out what was wrong with her, the more distant it all seemed. Soft lips pressed against her forehead in a chaste kiss and she suddenly realized she was horizontal again. But this time, she was on her back and moving…*Wow, who knew magic carpets wrapped around you before they took you from place to place?*

When she drifted back to herself again, Joelle realized she was sitting on someone and panicked. She flailed inside the cocoon of the blanket, trying to free herself from its confines. Strong arms banded tightly around her and she heard Brant's voice, "Settle down. I've got you, minx. Here, drink some of this." She hadn't managed to open her eyes yet, but she felt the straw he pressed against her lips. Taking a big drink, she was surprised by the tangy taste of orange juice. "Good girl, now relax for a few minutes. I just want to hold you—can you do that for me?" Joelle tried to nod her head but wasn't sure she'd succeeded. Letting everything fade into the background once again, she let go and slid into the darkness.

RYAN MORGAN HANDED his cousin a beer then settled into one of the chairs facing the sofa where Brandt sat with the beautiful redhead he'd punished—if that's what you wanted to call it. Nate had explained the circumstances and Ryan understood Brandt's strategy, but he and Big had laughed about the effectiveness of a punishment that involves an orgasm so intense it probably registered on the Richter scale.

He'd met Joelle Phillips at a party when he worked for Templar Enterprises Group's Security Division. Even though they'd been formally introduced, he had only gotten to speak to her briefly—but she'd certainly made an impression. He'd planned to call her after that first meeting, but work obligations had made it impossible. *Who would have ever imagined Miss Formal, Heiress to Phillips Pharmaceuticals would be into the kink scene?*

"You're early." Brandt never had been one to beat around the bush, a trait shared by most Special Forces operators. But, in Brandt's case it could easily be a genetic trait—*yeah, we Morgans aren't typically known for being suave.* Ryan didn't answer, he just nodded in agreement and grinned. "Christ, I don't know why I didn't think about you and Big being friends."

Big was walking behind the sofa and smacked the back of Brandt's head. "Watch it Star Boy, that badge doesn't give you the right to disrespect me in my own club." Ryan snorted a laugh, it was this sort of comradery he'd missed these last few months as he'd finished up his Residency. His classmates had been nice enough, just young and naïve. They'd also been cutthroat competitive, something that had grated on Ry's nerves. After years spent working as a part of a team—where your life depended on *every* member's success, he'd had little tolerance for their games. Ryan didn't regret the time he'd devoted to serving his country, he'd benefited from the experience in more ways than he'd probably ever know. But he'd seen a lot of the worst the world had to offer and those experiences had a way of changing a man.

Brandt rolled his eyes at Big's comment. "Hell, I know why you're waiting to go up to Pine Creek." Ryan started grinning like a fucking loon and Brandt knew he'd nailed it. "Just so you know, they left last night. Did Dad know you were holding back?" Ryan wanted to laugh out loud, he and his uncle had been talking at least once a week for months. Ryan loved his Aunt Patsy, but damn she could steamroll the most stubborn among them. Ryan wanted to view the town and medical facilities without being subjected to the family dynamo's hard sell techniques.

"You aren't the only one who called me about Doc "Slow" wanting to retire—and when I find out which one of you gave that crotchety old fart my phone number, there's going to be hell to pay." Ryan knew the elderly doctor hadn't told any of his patients the real reason he was planning to retire, and Ry had promised he wouldn't share the grim diagnosis Doc had gotten a few months back. Nodding toward Joelle, Ryan asked, "So, tell me how a world renowned medical researcher like Joelle Phillips ends up in a kink club in Montana?"

Ryan became aware of several things at the exact same instant. First, Joelle was no longer snoozing, he'd seen her muscles stiffen at his question. Second, neither Brandt nor Big appeared to know what the hell he was talking about. And third, his cousin was fucking furious—although Ryan wasn't entirely sure why. Phoenix stepped up behind Brandt as Ryan asked the question, his eyes going wide. Ryan was betting Brandt's younger brother knew more about Joelle than the Sheriff—and wasn't that going to go over like a lead fucking balloon? *Real smooth, man. Hell, no wonder my residency mentor kept saying my bedside manner needed work.*

Chapter Four

BRANDT SAW PHOENIX in one of the club's many mirrors when he stepped up behind him. At Ryan's question, his younger brother's eyes widened in guilt and he'd attempted to meld back into the shadows, but Brandt wasn't having it. "Don't even think about it, little brother."

Phoenix's muttered, "Fuck" was all he needed to hear. Obviously, his little brother already knew all or part of what Ryan just said—it was unlike one of his brothers to keep something like this secret, so Brandt was more than a little interest in his explanation.

The woman in his arms also reacted to Ryan's comment letting him know she'd recovered enough to realize there was trouble brewing. He leaned down, speaking against her ear, "I know you're awake, minx. You might as well open those pretty gray eyes. I'm interested in hearing the answer to Master Ryan's question myself." Her eyelids fluttered open, her apprehension easy to see. Under different circumstances, Brandt might have enjoyed seeing her uncertainty, but as it was—he wasn't happy to know she was so unsure of his reaction she looked like she was a half second from bolting.

Nate leaned forward, resting his forearms on his knees and spoke softly, "JoJo, I can only think of one reason I shouldn't kick you out of my club for lying on your application—are you in danger?" Joelle seemed to instinctively recognize what Brandt and Ryan both already knew, the cold tone of Nate Ledek's voice was not something she should ignore. The man had deadly accurate instincts, stories about the former SEAL's "calm before the storm" awareness were legendary among the club's members. Many attributed his ability to sense what was coming to his Native American ancestry, but Brandt had always believed Nate's true *gift* was his ability to read people. He understood their motivations, so he was better prepared to predict their behavior—and his quick assessment of the current situation was proof of how easily Nate could see through smoke and mirrors.

Joelle sat up still clutching the blanket around her and glanced between the three men she could see. "Can we talk about this upstairs? This isn't a conversation I'm comfortable having out in the open. And I'd like to get dressed first, also." Brandt agreed, but it didn't mean he wasn't reluctant to let her go at the door of the women's locker room. Her defeated expression and the complete lack of affect in her words worried him—the last thing he wanted was for her to run.

"Come straight up to Nate's office, minx." When she didn't meet his gaze, he used his fingers to lift her chin. "Don't even think about trying to skip out on us. Nate will have already seen that coming and you'll only get yourself into trouble if you try it." When her breath hitched, he knew he'd been right. "I'm guessing you think you're brave by handling whatever this is by yourself. But, sweetheart, sometimes the bravest thing you can do is ask for help."

He leaned forward and kissed her on the tip of her nose. "Don't forget that, minx. Now scoot. You've got five minutes. If you aren't in Nate's office on time, we'll be looking for you. And three former SEALs will be damned hard to hide from." He pushed the door open and turned her before giving her tender backside a sharp swat. Smiling to himself at her gasp, he headed upstairs.

RYAN STOOD WHEN Brandt walked through the door. "Hey, man, I'm sorry. I had my head up my ass after watching the scene." Pushing his fingers through his short hair in frustration, he shook his head. "Listen, before she gets up here, I want to tell you what I've heard. Word in the medical community is Joelle Phillips made a major discovery related to cancer treatment, but she was shut down by the Phillips Pharmaceuticals Board of Directors. Several of those board members have major holdings in companies who would take a big hit if her discovery becomes public. The last I heard no one knew where she was."

"Until now." Joelle's soft voice sounded from the door, how she'd managed to enter without them hearing her was anybody's guess. *Jesus, three fucking former Special Forces operatives in the room and a medical researcher gets the drop on us? When Ryan gets settled in Pine Creek, we need to spend some time training.* Brandt hated the thought of losing his edge, the world was changing in ways most Americans couldn't fathom, and letting down his guard wasn't anywhere in his plan.

Perhaps it was presumptuous to assume Ryan would decide to take over for Doc, but Brandt didn't think so. And judging from the way his cousin's eyes softened when he looked at Joelle, he and Ryan were going to be reviewing a conversation they had several years ago very soon. One night after sharing a ménage scene in their favorite Berlin kink club, they'd both lamented how difficult it was going to be to keep a woman happy given their post military career choices. Ryan planned to return to finish the last of his medical training and Brandt wanted to pursue a career in law enforcement. Both of their choices would keep them away from home more often than not, making it difficult to maintain a happy home life.

When Ryan suggested sharing a wife Brandt had laughed out loud, but Ryan's reminder about their friends Kent and Kyle West's parents had made him reconsider. The more they'd discussed it, the more plausible it had seemed despite the obvious cultural problems they anticipated. The entire conversation came back to Brandt in the span of a few heartbeats as he watched Ryan step forward and clasp Joelle's hands between his own. "Joelle, I want to apologize for how poorly I handled things downstairs."

Brandt was relieved to see the lost expression she'd had when he'd first looked up, fade as Ryan spoke. "Please don't worry, I should have known this would happen at some point. I've enjoyed the anonymity longer than I'd originally hoped I would be able to. Although I have to admit, I didn't anticipate being *outted* in this particular venue." His heart stuttered at her attempt to make light of the situation because it was easy to hear the sadness in her voice. A BDSM club was supposed to be a safe place to *be yourself* and tonight's disaster had stolen that from her.

Brandt stepped forward, turning her so she faced him. "Don't. Don't try to cover up your sadness with humor, minx. Not only is it not working, but it's only going to increase your anxiety and piss off the Doms in the room." He saw the moment she realized the truth of his words, her gray eyes darkened and her gaze dropped to the floor. Brandt tilted her chin up, hoping he could help her strike a balance between being open and honest while also staying respectful to herself as well as the men in the room since they were all intent on helping her.

After settling on the soft leather sofa, Master Nate handed her a bottle of water, his unspoken order clear. Joelle took several gulping drinks before recapping the bottle and setting it on the low table in front of her. She was grateful for the few seconds it had afforded her to get her thoughts in order. She didn't want them to think she was hiding her feelings or that she was in denial. Looking at Brandt, she spoke deliberately. "I understand, and I don't mean to be disrespectful, but you have to remember I was raised by a father who didn't suffer weakness well. He was loving, but he didn't believe coddling served any purpose. Fear and uncertainty were seen as weaknesses that needed to be concealed or they'd be used against you."

She hated seeing the looks of sympathy on their faces, this was exactly why she rarely opened up to anyone about her father. It would be wrong to say he didn't care about her—he absolutely did, in his own limited way. Joelle counted her blessings every single day because her life could have certainly been far different had her father chosen to leave her in the care of boarding schools like so many of her friends' parents had done. Instead, he'd taken an almost fanatical interest in her education, assuring her success was what you earned not what you inherited.

Phoenix was the one who finally broke the uncomfortable silence. "Why don't you tell us how you ended up in Pine Creek? And sweetheart, you need to make sure it's the whole story and not the abbreviated version you told me when you wanted the upgraded security system installed."

Joelle knew without asking Phoenix had done his homework. *Damn, he probably knows more about me than I do.*

Looking at the four men watching her, Joelle had a flash of the old movies where glaring spotlights were pointed at a woman tied to a chair. The intense lights blinding her to the deep, mysterious voices barking questions from beyond her view. They might not be shouting their inquiries, but their body language told her they intended to wring every detail from her. Taking a deep breath, Joelle started by explaining exactly what her position at Phillips Pharmaceuticals had been, and how important the research element had been to her personally. Having lost her mother to cancer as a young child, Joelle had been driven by the desire to prevent other kids from suffering the same loss.

"I'll spare you all the chemical details, but the important thing is the formula showed remarkable potential from the very beginning. And by the time I'd refined it, the results were truly astonishing. Best of all it's almost entirely organic so the number of people who won't tolerate the treatment it will be a fractional sample." She paused for a few seconds trying to refocus on the story because her emotions were starting to get involved. The potential for her discovery was so enormous, Joelle honestly had trouble understanding how the board could ignore the social responsibility accompanying a discovery of this magnitude.

"At what point did you share your findings with your father and the board?" Phoenix asked a question she suspected he already knew the answer to. But, she was grateful he'd brought her focus back to recounting the facts. It was so easy to get bogged down in the emotional quagmire of the board's rejection, and going down that road wasn't going to help.

"The results were well documented before I shared them. There wasn't any question but that we'd found a formula that could change the entire landscape of cancer treatment. To be honest, I was completely blown away by their response. Sure, I knew there would be factions of the medical community that wouldn't be thrilled. After all, we're talking about a multi-billion dollar industry. I wasn't naïve enough to think there wouldn't be huge financial implications. But I was completely unprepared for the vehemence of their reaction." Her dad had supported her but in the end, the board's demand she scrap the project remained. "Of course, I tried to make it appear as though I'd accepted their decision but truthfully I'm not a very good actress." Glancing at Nate, she grimaced. "As you may have already noticed."

Joelle felt her cheeks heat in embarrassment, and they felt like they'd been set on fire when Master Nate chuckled. But his words warmed her heart, "Darling girl, being genuine is a blessing. It's only a curse when you try to lie to yourself and those around you. Don't ever try to change who you are." She nodded her acknowledgment of his words but knew if she spoke there would be no way to contain the emotion.

The entire evening had been a roller coaster ride and she could feel the crash coming—and she certainly didn't want to hit bottom in front of these men. "I know this conversation isn't finished, but the truth is I'm not sure I can finish it tonight. It's been an emotional day, and I need to step back and regroup." Looking at each man individually, she noted the differences in their expressions and she was pleased they weren't trying to mask their feelings. Nate looked at her like a concerned older brother, it was remarkably similar to the look she'd seen in Phoenix's eyes during their collaboration on her security system. Tonight Phoenix's look was more compassionate as if he sensed how close she was to an emotional edge.

But it was the similar looks on Brandt and Ryan's faces that sent blazing sexual heat coursing through her system. She remembered meeting Ryan at a party several weeks before the debacle that sent her life into a tailspin. He'd had the same look in his eyes that night, but he'd been working so they hadn't been able to act on their mutual attraction. They'd only spoken briefly, but had managed to exchange contact information. From what she heard later, he'd left the country a few days after the party for an assignment in England, and before he'd returned she'd fled. There was definitely something unfinished between them, the attraction was undeniable, but it was also unsettling because she would be lying to herself to deny her attraction to Brandt.

Brandt's intensity was a *force* in itself…something a person had to experience to really understand. Their sexual chemistry was off the chart, but it was his underlying air of protectiveness that called to her. She'd seen it time and time again in his dealings with the citizens of Pine Creek. Despite his gruff exterior, everyone she'd met seemed to respect him. They'd all cited his military service, but there were also added tidbits about how he'd gone out of his way to help someone. Hell, she'd heard all about the hometown hero before they'd even met. She'd half expected him to be dressed in some sort of superhero costume and his entrance heralded by a dramatic sound tract. The day he'd walked in to the drug store in faded jeans, scuffed boots, and a flannel shirt, Joelle felt as if the air in the room had suddenly become electrified and she hadn't even been introduced to him yet.

The resemblance between Brandt and his brothers was strong enough that she'd been fairly certain he was one of the Morgan brothers. But, since she hadn't met them all at that point, she wasn't certain which one he was because he hadn't been in uniform. But as she watched him walk toward the counter where she was standing, the afternoon sun backlighting him, everything inside her went still. His eyes were locked on hers, and even though she didn't know why he was there, Joelle knew at that moment he was going to be important to her in some way. Even now, thinking back Joelle remembered how strongly she'd been attracted to him, and how the air around her had seemed to sizzle in anticipation as he approached her.

She'd felt the same electrically charged zing tonight during their scene. He'd tailored the scene to match her offense rather than simply administering a spanking or caning. Instead of doing what would have been easier and more expedient, Brandt had taken the time to get into her head, forcing her to face two fears that had been holding her back in club play for years. No other Dom had ever been able to get into her head. Hell, none of the Doms she'd played with had come even remotely close to earning her emotional submission. Surrendering her body to the moment had always been easy, but she'd never been able to fully submit mentally. That disconnection kept her from putting herself fully in a Dom's hand, and she'd never been able to let go and be vulnerable enough to orgasm in front of strangers…until tonight.

Standing, Joelle smiled but knew it wouldn't fool anyone. "I'll just grab my things and head out, it's late and I'd like to get home before dawn." The only part of the lifestyle Joelle had ever found challenging was the late hours. Clubs were notorious for catering to night owls...something she'd never been.

"Sit. Down." Ryan's sharp tone surprised her so much she plopped back down before her mind fully processed his command. She blinked in surprise, but he didn't miss a beat. "Joelle, you are obviously exhausted—both physically and emotionally." She looked on as he turned to Nate, they seemed to share some sort of unspoken communication and at the end, Nate nodded once. *Very strange indeed*. Ryan turned to Brandt and asked, "Is there any reason you can't stay down here tonight? You could drive Joelle back to Pine Creek in the morning and I'd follow you in her car."

Joelle felt her breath hitch at the implication. Again she felt there was a lot of silent communication taking place, but this time, Phoenix was watching with obvious interest as well. Ryan studied her for long seconds before returning his focus to Brandt. "Berlin?" *Well, at least, they are using words now...sort of.*

"Yes." Brandt hadn't hesitated, his answer quick and sure, then he'd smiled before turning to Phoenix, handing him a small key ring. "There is a go bag in the trunk. Send it in with the valet, he can make sure it gets upstairs. I'll send Beck a message letting him know he'll be on call until we get home tomorrow." Joelle knew Brandt was referring to his part-time deputy and she hoped this wouldn't be a problem for the other man, after all, he had a new baby at home.

Phoenix nodded but didn't leave. Instead, he turned to her. "Are you okay with this, sweetheart?" She understood what he was asking...he wanted to be absolutely certain she understood what his brother and Ryan were proposing. Oh, she a pretty good idea. She might not know all the particulars, but their intent seemed fairly straightforward to her. What she didn't understand was why it didn't bother

her. Shouldn't she be outraged at the suggestion of staying with two men? For some reason, she couldn't think of a single reason to turn down their invitation. When she finally managed to nod, Phoenix shook his head, "You know better, sweetheart. I need to hear the words."

Joelle swallowed hard making sure her voice would sound convincing. She and Phoenix had become friends, and she knew if he sensed any trepidation on her part he'd drive her home himself. "I'll be fine, Phoenix. Thank you for your concern." When he pulled her into a hug, she whispered against his ear, "The only thing at risk is my pride…and maybe my heart."

When he pulled back, he shook his head. "Actually, I think it might well be the other way around." Grinning, he leaned forward and pressed a chaste kiss against her forehead. "I'll check in with you tomorrow. Be careful with my brother and cousin, they pout if they don't get to be the boss." *Cousin? Oh, Lord. Didn't that just figure?* She knew they had the same last name, but Morgan was a fairly common name. *And hadn't Ryan told her he was originally from Texas?*

"Please be careful driving home, it's awfully late." Phoenix gave her a sharp salute and then walked out the door.

Master Nate looked at her and smiled before turning to Ryan and Brandt. "Make sure you explain where *everything* is upstairs." She wasn't sure what he could be referring to, but obviously, both men understood.

"She'll be safe in our care, Big, you know that."

"See to it she is." Master Nate was definitely back in residence. He turned to her, "If you need anything, anything at all, just dial zero or hit the panic alarm and someone from my staff will be there in short order to help." *Panic alarm?* He didn't wait for her to respond, turning on his heel, he left through the same door Phoenix used. Joelle wasn't sure what she'd expected to happen next, but she was surprised by how quickly both men moved in front of her. Each taking one of her hands they pulled her to her feet in a move so well coordinated she'd have thought it had been choreographed if she didn't know better.

"Come on, minx, let's get you settled before you crash." Brandt and Ryan turned and began moving toward the door not wasting any time with chitchat. *So much for romance.*

FORMER SENATOR HELEN Rodrick stood in front of the bank of floor to ceiling windows in the hotel's VIP suite, her arms crossed over her chest as the stared out into the fading sunlight. She'd been quietly looking for Joelle Phillips for the past year and it finally looked as though the elusive young researcher had been located. It would have been much faster to track the woman on-line, but Helen knew too well how easily those inquiries could have been traced back to her.

What Joelle was doing in a small town in Montana wasn't clear, but it seemed unlikely the brilliant young scientist had randomly chosen the location. People like Ms. Phillips didn't *do random*—they were meticulous in their actions. The challenge Helen had was deciphering the young woman's thinking. If she'd stayed in that location this long, then chances were she had support there and it was certainly something that needed to be taken into consideration.

Helen's Presidential candidacy had already been plagued by controversy; the last thing she needed was to have it further crippled by allegations she'd intentionally helped suppress a potential cancer cure for personal financial gain. Hell, she was already battling never-ending criticism over her past associations with the world's financial titans. She'd been planning this candidacy for years and she damned well wouldn't see her moment in history undermined because some other woman had aspirations of ending one of the world's most financially profitable medical conditions. When Helen's financial backers had gotten wind of rumors surrounding Phillips Pharmaceuticals' pending breakthrough her phone had blown up with calls, texts, and email from around the world.

When her phone pinged with an incoming message, Helen turned to pick up the device she was beginning to think owned her rather than the other way around. *Info is probably in her house since the place is secured far better than any home in BFE needs.*

Why else would she secure a small home in bum fuck Egypt as her chief of security had so eloquently put it? Helen agreed the woman's formula notes were likely hidden in her home, now all her hired muscle needed to do was get in and out without being detected by the local sheriff. And everything she'd read indicated the man was remarkably capable considering he lived in one of the least populated areas of the country. Of course, former Navy SEALs were never incompetent and this one was a local so he was even more dedicated to protecting the citizens in his jurisdiction.

Tapping out a reply, Helen kept her long-range plans for Ms. Phillips to herself. *Can you secure the information without alerting local LE?* Over the years, Helen had discovered local law enforcement could be surprising alert to strangers in their communities, and the last thing she needed was to be tied to a burglary in Montana.

His didn't respond for several long seconds letting her know he was choosing his words carefully. *If it's there, we'll find it. Sophisticated systems require specialists.* So he was calling in someone else, meaning she was going to have to wait...definitely not her strongest personality trait. There were several individuals on the Phillips board who would also take a significant financial hit should Joelle Phillips decide to go public, so it was unlikely the break in would be tied solely to her. Helen had no plans to turn loose what was a potential financial windfall of unimaginable proportions. *No, that formula isn't going to see the light of day until I've gotten everything in place and then I'll bask happily in the spotlight since it will become public after I take office.*

PHOENIX MADE GREAT time driving home. Damn it was fun to drive full out. Once he hit the county line, it was balls to the wall since he knew the local sheriff was otherwise occupied. He decided to drive by Joelle's place and double check the newest alarm system he'd activated around the perimeter of her property. The new sensors would likely need to be tweaked because they were more sensitive than most and local wildlife was common on the outskirts of town. The property Joelle inherited was definitely far enough from the center of town to have its share of four-legged visitors. He was ten minutes from her home when his phone pinged with an alert indicating the rear perimeter had been breached. *Damn it, I know better than to think shit*

into existence. I should have just blanked it from my mind and gone home.

Accelerating, Phoenix hit the speed dial for Kip and was grateful his when his younger brother answered on the first ring. "This better be fucking earth shattering—what?" The youngest Morgan had never been particularly cheerful when he first woke up. Hell, Phoenix would enjoy stoking the fire of Kips' surliness if he didn't need his help.

"Get to Joelle's. Alarm going off around the back perimeter. Might be critters, but I don't think so. There was a guy on the front steps late yesterday afternoon. Video picked him up, he was too interested in the decoy equipment in my opinion." He could hear Kip moving around, but hadn't heard his truck start yet—and there wasn't a chance in hell he'd have missed it. Kip hadn't yet outgrown his monster truck and there was no mistaking the massive diesel engine's distinctive roar. When he heard a soft, feminine voice ask Kip where he was going, Phoenix wanted to roll his eyes. *Damn, that boy is a fucking magnet for sweet women—hell, all women.* Kip said something about a family emergency a second before Phoenix heard a door slam.

"I'll be there in two minutes." Kip's truck roared to life and for the first time, Phoenix was grateful his kid brother's vehicle was loud enough to alert everyone within a mile radius he was moving. As nice as it would be to catch the intruder, neither of them was the best choice to make a capture despite the fact he was sure both vehicles had weapons stashed inside.

Hell, Kip was like an untrained bird dog—he'd eat the prey before Brandt could take possession. And Phoenix's experience with violence was limited to the wildly successful digital games he created. A second alarm pinged letting

Phoenix know whoever triggered the first sensor had probably heard Kip's truck and was on the move. Hopefully, the video equipment got a decent shot of the intruder.

"Not even going to ask where you were. We're going to roll in at about the same time—Brandt's still at the club." Phoenix didn't have to see Kip to know he'd surprised him.

"Wanna catch me up?" Kip's voice held a note of amusement that was easy enough to hear. The youngest Morgan brother was always glad to have some of the sexual spotlight shining on someone else.

"I'll update you after we find out what's going on."

"Do you know if Joelle is home?"

"She isn't. She is at the club with Brandt and Ryan." Kip's chuckle sounded through the speakers as they both rounded the corner from opposite directions and barreled down the short drive into Joelle's front yard. "I got a second alarm, so I'd say whoever it was heard your approach and bailed." Disconnecting the call, Phoenix pulled up beside Kip and stepped out of the car.

"I heard a motor fire up behind the trees, but there's no way to get back there before whoever it was hits the highway. Besides, I haven't been up long enough to run that far." They started walking toward the house as Phoenix dialed Brandt—so much for the nap he'd been looking forward to. But knowing he was going to spoil Brandt and Ryan's plans made him grin, hell, why should those two have all the fun?

Chapter Five

JOELLE HADN'T EVEN gotten to sleep when Phoenix's call sent both Brandt and Ryan into hyper drive. *I thought SEALs were supposed to be super calm in the face of crises?* Both of them had "mobilized"...whatever the hell that meant, and rushed her out of the club so quickly her head had been spinning by the time they reached the club's sheltered parking area. Brandt had tossed her keys to Nate on the way out and they'd piled into Ryan's car.

They'd basically shoved her into the backseat of the silver Bentley Bentayga and been moving before she'd even fastened her seat belt. "Hold on, baby." *Yeah, no shit. A seat belt wasn't going to do any good, she'd be better off with a parachute the way they were flying down the road.* Joelle wasn't a gear head by any stretch of the imagination, but this happened to be a car she'd actually heard about. It was an amazing piece of automotive engineering for sure, and from what she could tell it probably doubled as a rocket. Her dad had always enjoyed expensive automobiles and this one more than qualified as expensive. But she had to admit, she was more than a little curious how a former SEAL, who'd only recently finished his residency could afford a car that had likely cost well over a quarter million dollars.

"Joelle, cinch your seatbelt tighter. Ry sometimes forgets he's in a car and not flying."

"Not true. I've never flown this close to trees. Trees fuck you up when you hit them. I avoid them at all costs. Besides, I've got precious cargo in the backseat so I'm going to be careful." She could see his mischievous grin when he turned and winked at her over his shoulder before he shrugged. "But you might want to cinch up anyway, better to err on the side of the angels, baby." *Yeah, well thanks for the tip, but I'm already having trouble taking a deep breath I've got the damned thing so tight.* Evidently Brandt hadn't trusted her to tighten the strap herself because he reached around and gave the strap a hard yank causing her to gasp. Hell, she wasn't going to be able to feel her legs by the time they got back to Pine Creek.

Things were flying past in a blur and Joelle needed a distraction to keep the rising panic at bay. "This is a nice car, but I'm curious how you got your hands on one already. I didn't think it was supposed to be out for a few months."

Ryan grinned over his shoulder. "I've got connections." When she didn't take the bait, he shrugged and continued, "I've got friends in the oil industry and they called in favors. It was a graduation gift from my dad's company." Brandt laughed out loud earning him a glare from Ryan. The look didn't hold any real heat, and reminded her of the looks she and her roommate had shared in college when one of them said something absurd.

"We'll chat about Ry's parents later, minx, but suffice it to say, this bauble didn't even make the line-item list for their accountant." *What? Is he trying to be ambiguous?* Deciding to let it go, she leaned back and let the plush leather of the comfortable seat cradle the back of her head.

She tried to listen as Brandt spoke on the phone, but he was speaking in what she was sure was some mix of military and police code that wasn't meant to be understood by mere mortals. *Why do they do that? It's like they are purposely excluding anyone who isn't in their special club.* She'd have to get a decoder ring if she was going to care about such things, but right now she could barely manage even a flicker of interest.

She'd dealt with enough of that "exclusive club" mentality during her years in private schools to last her several lifetimes...she damned well wasn't playing the same asinine game as an adult. Before she could work herself up into a good "mad," Joelle felt her body relaxing despite her best efforts to fight the fatigue. The seat was warming around her and in less than a minute she felt the weight of sheer exhaustion pull her under. Joelle knew she was losing the battle to stay awake, but she couldn't work up the energy to care. Despite their ridiculous speed, the ride was smooth and she finally surrendered. Leaning against the side of the car, she let go and fell into a sweet abyss of sleep.

RYAN HAD SEEN the battle between fear, frustration, and fatigue waging in Joelle's eyes and knew the heated seat would help her body's need for rest win the war. He smiled to himself at how quickly she'd fallen asleep despite the fact she was strapped in the back of a car rocketing down the highway at an obscene speed.

"Might as well throttle this beast back. Phoenix said the perp slipped through the trees and escaped." Brandt rubbed his hands over his face in frustration. "You know, a part of me is pissed they missed him—no doubt Kip's fucking truck alerted two thirds of the people in the county he was headed in that direction. But a bigger part of me is relieved because who knows what they were barreling into."

"And that really isn't their area of expertise—despite the fact I'm sure they were well armed." Ryan didn't try to hold back his chuckle. Hell, his cousins had all been born and raised on a ranch so guns had been a part of their lives since they were old enough to hold them. It hadn't come as a surprise to anyone who knew Brandt when he qualified for sniper training. Even though he was a skilled marksman, killing hadn't come easy to him and the man he loved like a brother had paid a huge emotional price for his time as a SEAL.

Brandt hadn't talked to Ryan about what went down on that last mission, but the scuttlebutt among the teams had provided more than enough information. Ryan knew how difficult Brandt's battle with PTSD had been because he'd stayed in close contact with his Uncle Dean and his other cousins during the past year. Ryan had encouraged them to be patient and supportive, assuring them Brandt would fight his way back to the surface soon enough. There had been times when he'd wondered if he hadn't led them astray, but from the looks of things now, Brandt was definitely on the mend. *Funny how the right woman at the right time can make all the difference.*

"Oh I'm sure they both had weapons with them, but I'd like to talk to whoever was there. Phoenix might have managed some restraint if the adrenaline didn't kick his control to the curb. But Kip? Hell, he probably wouldn't realize what he was feeling was an adrenaline rush, and he damned sure wouldn't feel a moment's remorse. You pull him out of a woman's bed at this hour, that boy is gonna shoot first and ask questions sometime next week." Brandt's sly grin assured Ryan the ornery kid he'd once known was still inside the morose man they'd all worried about for the past year and a half. Relief flooded him as he realized their crazy plan to share a woman might actually work.

He'd always worried he wouldn't find a woman who would be willing to put up with the brutally demanding schedule of doctors in rural areas. But, Ryan had never wanted to specialize in some boring peripheral branch of medicine just to ensure he rarely worked anything but normal office hours. After spending several summers in Pine Creek, he'd always dreamed of settling into a small town—there was something about the intimacy of knowing everyone in the community that seemed *right* to him.

A single trip to the Pine Creek Emergency Room when he'd been sixteen was still burned in his memory. He and his cousins had been racing dirt bikes up the mountain trails behind their home when Ryan rounded a corner ahead of Kip to find a couple of hikers directly in front of him. Despite the fact he knew they were trespassing, his instinct to protect the young couple kicked in making him jerk the bike sharply to the left. The move sent him tumbling end over end down the rocky embankment.

His injuries had been serious enough the first responders on the scene hadn't wanted to take a chance transporting him to a larger hospital in Missoula or Billings, taking him instead to the much smaller facility in Pine Creek. The medical center would more accurately be described as an elaborate clinic. Their equipment had been dated, but the elderly physician who'd treated him had been top notch. The old man hadn't missed a thing, he'd even properly diagnosed Ryan's lacerated liver. And, rather than following the old standard treatment recommendation for emergency surgery, the well-read physician opted to stall and monitor Ryan's lab tests vigilantly giving his body time to heal the wound on its own. The move had saved Ryan weeks of recovery time and impressed the specialists he'd seen after returning home to Texas.

Doc had stayed at his bedside for thirty-six hours straight, not trusting anyone else to notice the subtle changes he'd assured Dean and Patsy Morgan he was watching for. His dedication to a teenager who'd been driving recklessly and over-reacted causing the fall had been a turning point in Ryan's young life. Late one night after Doc had finally agreed to release him the next morning, Ryan tried to thank the physician for all he'd done. "Sir, I don't know how to thank you, well, for everything. But mostly for assuring my mom and dad I'm going to be okay. I didn't want them coming home from their trip—they'd been looking forward to this for a long time."

The old guy hadn't responded, he'd just looked at Ryan over the top of his glasses for long seconds. He'd finally folded the half-moon spectacles and slid them into his pocket before leaning back against the small sink in the corner of the room. "The best way to repay someone for a kindness is to pass it along three-fold. It's just another take on the Rule of Three, which says everything—both good and bad, that you do comes back to you times three. So if you repeat my kindness three times and each of those people do the same—the world becomes a better place in a real big hurry." It had been a defining moment and from that point forward, Ryan's life had changed direction. He'd always assumed he'd join his father in the energy industry, but everything had been different after that summer.

Bringing his thoughts back to the moment, Ryan glanced over his shoulder, he smiled. "She captivates me.

She did the first time I met her, but work kept me from following up after we were introduced."

"Don't take this the wrong way—but I'm damned glad. If that hadn't happened, I might not have ever met her." The sincerity in Brandt's expression only served to reinforce what Ryan had already seen—if his cousin wasn't already in love with Joelle, he was definitely moving in that direction. The next time Brandt spoke, his words were much quieter, as if he didn't want to wake the woman sleeping quietly behind him. "Both of us have chosen careers that will keep us away from home more than we'd like. And, we've already discussed sharing. I know it was a long time ago, but…"

"Yes." He let the one word response sit between them for several seconds before continuing. "If you're asking if I'm still interested in a polyamorous relationship, the answer is an unequivocal, resounding *yes*. I don't know how Joelle will feel about it, but I'm damned anxious to find out. I'm sure you feel the same way I do about her safety. I'd like to see this mess resolved before we add any unnecessary stress to her life."

"Agreed." Brandt paused so long, Ryan thought the conversation was over. But then he saw a knowing grin spread over his cousin's face. "I assume this means Pine Creek is going to have another Doc soon?"

Ryan didn't hesitate, laughing he answered, "Hell, your dad sealed this deal weeks ago. This visit is just a formality. I was going to try to find a place while I was here, but now I'm thinking maybe we ought to all stay at the ranch—at least for a while." God knew there was plenty of space in the main house. He'd also heard several of his cousins' homes were finished or nearly so, there should be plenty of options available.

"Joelle definitely needs to stay at the ranch until we get this sorted out. Phoenix is probably ramping up the security system he installed at her place, but nothing beats layers of protection and she'll have it at the ranch. And we might actually get spend some quality time with her without being interrupted if we have your brothers watching our backs. Hell, I want to shoot the bastard who tripped the alarm for fucking up our time with her if nothing else." Ryan didn't care if he sounded petulant, he'd been looking forward to spending some time with Joelle between them even if it was just to sleep for a few hours. He'd been intrigued by her when they first met and now—knowing they shared an in interest in dominance and submission? Hell, he could hardly wait to explore the lifestyle with her, and adding Brandt into the mix the frosting on the cake.

BRANDT LOOKED AT his cousin and grinned. "Understood. I have a lot of pent up frustration waiting on the fucker trying to hurt her myself. And screwing up my aftercare plans didn't do anything to improve my mood. As you know, my team's last mission, well, it went so far south I saw a penguin sporting a Timberwolf C14." His favored sniper rifle might not be as recognizable as some others, but it had never failed him. It didn't matter his Commanding Officer taunted that he'd chosen it simply because of the name—hell, maybe there had been a thread of truth to his accusation. But when his life and those of his team depended on him being able to feel as though the rifle was an extension of himself, he didn't question *why* something worked—he just used it.

"The whole operation was FUBAR from the time we hit the ground and I'm itching to set a few things straight with the Universe." Fucked up beyond all recognition was a gross understatement, hell, the enemy had been waiting for them. Brandt never was able to find out all the details, but he knew clear to his toes they'd been set up.

As they neared Joelle's home, he turned to wake her and saw she was already looking out the window. He hated seeing the forlorn look in her eyes and wished like hell he wasn't sure he knew what she was thinking. "Joelle, Phoenix and Kip have already cleared the yard, but they're waiting for me to get there before entering the house." It was several seconds before she met his gaze—she didn't respond, just waited patiently for him to continue. "Is the alarm system the only thing we need to contend with?"

She blinked at him in confusion for a few seconds before he saw understanding dawn in her eyes. "Are you asking me if I've booby-trapped the place?" When he nodded, her soft laugh didn't reflect even a hint of humor. "No. I know Coral said she'd done that in her apartment, but with Phoenix's security system in place, glassware in front of the door seemed like overkill." He was glad to see she was, at least, pretending her sense of humor was returning, even though he could see the resignation in her eyes. Damn, he hated knowing she thought running was her only option. It wasn't—not by a long shot, but he was equally convinced it wasn't going to be easy to persuade her otherwise.

Before stepping out of the vehicle, Brandt gave Ryan a knowing look—the message clear. *Take care of her.* He joined his brothers and listened as they relayed what they'd found. After listening to Kip describe where he'd heard a vehicle roar to life, there wasn't any question the perimeter breach had been intentional. No one *accidentally* ended up in the rutted woods behind Joelle's home. The area was covered in thick brush and riddled with treacherous washouts tourists wouldn't find and locals didn't have any interest in dealing with. Hell, everyone knew it had been part of the reason Joelle's reclusive uncle had liked the property so much and he assumed it was also a factor in Joelle staying in Pine Creek. She'd probably felt safer in a location knowing she only needed to secure the house itself.

It didn't take long to determine Phoenix's security system had not been compromised, but it didn't mean Brandt wanted Joelle to stay there alone. Even with Brandt and Ryan staying with her, Joelle wouldn't be as safe in her home as she'd be at the ranch. Not only was the ranch house secured by a state of the art system including a safe room with a secondary escape route, more importantly, but there were also more people around. At any given time, there were probably a dozen people milling around the area surrounding the house.

Ryan helped Joelle out of the car when they saw Brandt headed their way—she surprised him by stepping forward and meeting his gaze. "I'm not going to be able to stay here now, am I?" Well, at least, it looked as if they were going to be able to skip the first part of the argument he'd worried about.

"No, sweetheart, I don't think that would be wise."

Before he could finish, she turned to Ryan. "After your meetings today, do you think you could take me back to the club to get my car? I'll spend the day packing and hopefully I can find a moving company with a temporary storage facility." Neither Brandt nor Ryan interrupted her, she needed a chance to vent, even though she was wasting energy trying to sort through everything. He'd seen a lot of reactions to trauma and learned a long time ago to let victims work through the bursts of emotion that followed whatever way they could. Logic could wait now that the imminent danger had passed.

Chapter Six

JOELLE LOOKED AROUND the massive kitchen in the Morgan family home marveling at how a room so large could still feel so cozy. She'd been in the Morgan's home for their annual New Year's Eve party…which turned out to also be night Sage Morgan proposed to her friend Coral. She also visited their home several times during the wedding festivities, and she was always in awe of the earthy elegance of the space. The Morgan's mountain mansion was such a contrast to the home Joelle had grown up in…her father's home was a marble and gilded gold monstrosity. It was beautiful in its own way, but it had always felt more like a museum than a home. Even as a child she'd known it wasn't a place she could relax.

Taking a deep breath, Joelle tried to sort through the quagmire of emotions she'd been swamped in since she'd realized the Dom Master Nate had assigned to punish her was none other than Brandt Morgan. God in fucking heaven…had it been less than twenty-four hours ago? How in the hell had her life completely derailed so quickly? Taking a deep breath, Joelle tried to focus her attention on the steaming cup of tea in front of her. She wasn't a fool, she knew Kip Morgan had used decaffeinated tea. She'd wanted to laugh at his attempt to dupe her—*hello there, sweetie, but I'm a chemist, and we notice things like our drug of choice missing from a beverage.*

After Ryan and Brandt politely explained they had no intention of helping her move from Pine Creek she'd tried to reason with them, but a couple of sharp swats to her tender behind served as a poignant reminder of why arguing with Doms was never a good idea. They'd promised to provide her a with a world class paddling right in her own front yard if she didn't stop babbling about moving and start packing whatever she'd need for the next few days. Joelle appreciated the fact they hadn't followed her around her house while she gathered up everything she needed. They'd probably known she had things hidden in her home...things she'd need to take with her and their respect for her privacy had gone a long way in convincing her to follow their damned edicts. *Yeah, and the fact they are both hot former Special Forces operatives trained to keep entire countries safe didn't play into it at all—get a grip, Joelle.*

One of the flash drives containing her information about the formula was nestled inside her purse. It wasn't an ideal hiding place, but it was better than taking a risk and leaving it behind. Joelle was still grateful for her uncle's series of clues that had eventually led her to the small safe hidden beneath the floorboards in her bedroom. Without the clues he'd left her, Joelle doubted she'd have ever found the in-floor safe. Her mother's only brother had obviously been more than a little paranoid, but he'd also been brilliant in his own way. The historical fiction books he'd written were so full of detail she knew he had to have spent years researching each of the novels he'd penned. And leaving the royalties from those books to the history department of a local college had been a gift she knew would fund several scholarships for years to come.

Joelle leaned her chin on her hand to keep from laying her head on the Morgan's kitchen table. She blinked her tired eyes in an attempt to bring her surroundings into focus while trying desperately to stay awake as five Morgan men discussed what *she* was going to do. *What the hell am I, fucking invisible?* God save her from a roomful of alpha males. If they kept yakking much longer, she was going to be comatose. Damn, she was tired. There was a small part of her that knew she was straddling a blurred line between being fully asleep and alert, but it seemed like too much effort to nit-pick so she let it go.

She felt her chin slip from her palm and yelped when it hit the table with a solid thump. *Damn, damn, damn, that hurt.* She was on her feet before she realized she'd even stood. The thump of her chin on the wood and the scraping of her chair across the floor drew the attention of the men across the room. Ryan was the first to reach her, his strong hands cupping her shoulders as she shook her head in an effort to push the exhaustion aside. Brandt stepped up to her, concern etching his gorgeous features…or at least, she thought it was concern. It was hard to tell because her vision was blurry from exhaustion. God, she needed to get some rest, since she couldn't even see clearly. Her attention shifted between Brandt and Ryan as she asked, "Can someone please show me to my room? I'm really tired."

Ryan tipped her chin up and running his fingers along the underside, and frowned. "Christ, at least, you didn't split it open. Stitching up this pretty face definitely wasn't in my plans for tonight."

Colt Morgan's voice sounded from across the table, "Yeah and it's all about you, Doc." The sarcasm in his voice was tinged with enough respect and humor to make Joelle smile. When she looked up at the second Morgan brother, his smile was sweetly indulgent. "Sweetie, please sit down before your knees fold out from under you." When she dropped back into her chair, he nodded. "Better. Now, if one of these jokers doesn't take you to Brandt's suite in the next couple of minutes I'll take you to one of the guest suites—how's that sound?"

"Thanks, I appreciate your hospitality." She saw the corners of his mouth turn up in a grin, and knew he was deliberately taunting his brother and cousin, but if it helped her find a place to crash she didn't care. She'd barely gotten the words out before Brandt scooped her up in his arms. Before they were out of the room her eyes were already drifting closed, but she heard him tell his brothers he'd be back as soon as he helped Ryan get her settled. Her curiosity flickered briefly but was quickly lost in the darkness of blessed sleep.

RYAN FOLLOWED BRANDT down the hall even though he knew exactly where they were going. The Morgan brothers had chosen their suites years earlier and the only one of them who'd moved was Sage. The eldest brother had taken over his parents' master suite in the other wing of the house when they moved into a house in town. Ryan knew his aunt and uncle planned to spend most of the year traveling so the smaller home in Pine Creek worked out fine. He knew they'd hoped their moving would bring a woman into Sage's life and damn if it didn't seem to have worked. It was just one more example of how intuitive Patsy Morgan had always been.

Ryan hadn't been able to attend Sage and Coral's Valentine's Day wedding, so he was looking forward to their return to Pine Creek in a couple of weeks. He hoped things were resolved with Joelle by that time. Not only was he anxious to know she was safe, but he also knew Sage wouldn't be happy knowing his new bride could be in danger because her friend was staying under the same roof. All four of the Morgan brothers had expressed similar concerns downstairs and even though he knew Joelle hadn't heard that part of their conversation, Ryan knew she'd come to the same conclusion herself soon enough.

Brandt set Joelle on the marble counter in the en suite bathroom while Ryan readied the shower. Moving her into the small room Brandt called a shower, Ryan was amazed at how much the water seemed to revive her. He'd hoped it would sooth the worry he sensed weighing heavily on her mind, but it seemed to have had the opposite effect. Ryan was working conditioner into her long hair when he heard Brandt growl a warning. "Minx, you keep that up and you're not going to get to sleep for a while, and my brothers are going to be left cooling their heels down in the kitchen longer than they'll appreciate."

"Well, that's a real shame because I was sort of hoping now that I'm awake you might like to help me burn off a little nervous energy." Ryan wanted to laugh, she was so blatantly topping from the bottom he couldn't help but roll his eyes at Brandt who was still standing behind her watching their interaction. Oh, they were going to help her work off some energy, all right—but he doubted seriously it was going to happen in the way she'd hoped.

He finished rinsing her hair and Brandt turned her to face him so he could run his soap-slicked hands over her breasts. Pulling her nipples into tight peaks, he watched a pink blush spread over her chest as her breathing hitched. Seems this sweet sub responded perfectly to a small bite of pain with her pleasure. *Damn, she is perfect for us.* Ryan wasn't a sadist by any means, but it didn't mean he didn't understand the intimate relationship between pleasure and pain. Hell, the two sensations were simply flip sides of the same coin and he knew Brandt was of a like mind. They had different skill sets when it came to play and he was anxious to introduce her to their favorite ways to bring a woman pleasure.

Focusing his attention on her breasts, Ryan continued his assault on her senses as Brandt soaped the rest of her delectable body. As she started to tremble and he wanted to shout out in victory. Damn, he loved the way she responded to his touch. The tangy sent of her arousal flooded his senses but he didn't want to use soap covered hands on the delicate tissues of her sex. The urge to slide his fingers between the silky petals of her pussy had him quickly rinsing the shower gel from his hands. "Widen your stance for me, baby. I want to touch you."

Her gray eyes were already clouding with desire, but her feet slid apart opening her sex to his touch. He watched Brandt wrap an arm around her, lifting her breasts until her nipples looked like they were trying to reclaim his attention. Ryan was grateful Brandt had anticipated her need for support because he intended to rob her of the ability to stand on her own when he sent her into orbit. Just as his fingers slid into the top of her slit, he leaned forward to take the lobe of her ear between his teeth. "Are you wet for me, baby? Are my fingers going to slide through your sweet honey?"

"Yes, sir." They hadn't told her this was a scene, but she'd automatically melted into the role. *Fucking perfect.*

God, she was slick and even without looking he knew her tissues were swollen, the pretty petals of her rose-colored pussy flowered open. He'd teased his former employers relentlessly about their use of red roses in the

Knights Club décor, it's thinly veiled likeness to female genitalia so blatantly obvious. It seemed to him there must have been something more subtle they could have used, but they'd simply laughed as they'd assured him if it was good enough for the Knights of the Round Table it was good enough for them.

"You are deliciously wet and perfectly wanton aren't you, baby? Absolutely perfect. Now, let's see if we can't take the edge off, shall we?" With well-practiced precision, Ryan slid his fingers through her wet sex, circling her clit on random passes—never using a predictable pattern. Keeping her on edge as long as possible would increase her pleasure, but he wasn't sure how long she was going to last, her soft cries were already filling the steam-fogged air around them.

Ryan watched Brandt lean forward to bite down gently on the tender place where her neck met her shoulder. Joelle's entire body shuddered in response and once again Ryan was pleased to see her reaction to such a small example of what they could give her. "Minx, you're killing me. I can hardly wait to fuck you. And preparing you to take us together is going to be the sweetest torture in the world. We'll fill you up so full you won't remember a moment we weren't a part of you." Joelle's moans of assent were barely audible in between her panting breaths. Ryan wasn't sure what part of their dual assault was spinning her up so quickly, but it was damned satisfying knowing the two of them could have this effect on her.

They'd met a few women over the years who were so emotionally uptight about participating in a ménage they'd never were able to truly let go and enjoy the experience. He'd always felt sorry for them—all those years of cultural brainwashing about socio-sexual taboos denied them the pleasure that could have been so easily theirs. But Joelle wasn't having any trouble enjoying this moment that was for sure, he didn't know how it would play out long-term, but he wasn't going to let that deny him this moment.

Pushing his middle finger into her channel, he was shocked at how tight she was. "Baby? When is the last time you were fucked?" Brandt's glare let Ryan know his cousin wasn't particularly pleased with his blunt approach—damn, he really *was* going to have to work on his communication skills. Growing up in Texas where blunt was equated with honesty and then years as a SEAL had eroded his ability to practice what his mother referred to as "social niceties." From what Ryan could derive, she'd been politely calling him a clod, but he was equally convinced she'd never tell him that directly.

During his time with Templar, he'd spent time with their women and they'd been working hard to "polish him"—their words, not his. But from the look on Brandt's face, Ryan was guessing they hadn't managed to make a significant difference. Hell, maybe he'd give Carli a call—she'd spent years gracing magazine covers around the world but you'd likely never find anyone more humble. Her younger sister, Cressi would simply tell him to cry in the truck or suck it up—she'd loved teasing him about his Texas twang. The women his bosses had claimed for themselves were both gorgeous and brilliant—much like the woman standing in front of him.

Watching Joelle come by their hands as pure rapture shook her entire body so violently Ryan wondered if she would break apart, was the most erotic thing he'd ever seen in his entire life. He'd visited kink clubs all over the world, but he'd never see anything more breathtaking than Joelle lost in those long seconds of complete abandon.

While Brandt patted her skin dry Ryan combed the tangles from her hair before securing it in a loose braid.

When Joelle opened her eyes and gave him a drowsy, but questioning look Ryan felt himself blush. He shrugged but finally answered her unspoken question. "You probably don't really want to know, but I don't want there to be questions between us. I had a girlfriend in high school who showed horses on the weekends. If I wanted to spend time with her, I had to tag along. She taught me to braid." What he left out was the fact he'd learned so she'd finish up sooner, those stolen moments behind the chutes and barns of various show arenas had proven to be a very fertile learning ground for a sixteen-year-old boy. He'd scored a nineteen-year-old girlfriend because he was the Morgan Oil heir and had a fleet of fancy vehicles at his disposal. The few months he dated Nikki had been a crash course in what he later termed as kink for beginners. He'd always be grateful for all she taught him.

Joelle's dove gray eyes softened and her sweet smile was a relief. "How old were you?"

Ryan felt himself cringe as Brandt chuckled behind her. "Sixteen. But she was nineteen and far more sexually advanced than I was—although I did prove to be a quick study and caught up pretty quickly."

This time, she giggled softly. "I'll just bet you did. Perhaps I should thank her…seems I might be on the winning end of her tutelage." Ryan didn't answer, he just nodded and turned her to Brandt.

"I'm going downstairs for a few minutes. I want to call Sage and give him a quick update since they'd talked about coming home early. I'll also call Micah Drake and Jax McDonald at the Prairie Winds Club—those two are pure magic at digging up dirt and I have a feeling somebody on the Phillips BOD is hot to keep your discovery suppressed." Ryan agreed, but something about the whole situation didn't ring true to him and he hadn't been able to put his finger on it yet. His gut told him there was more at stake than a few shares of stock, what he didn't know *yet* was *who* or *what*. He agreed Kent and Kyle West's security team was top-notch. Hell, he wasn't too sure they weren't better connected than the men at Templar.

Ryan hoped Brandt and Joelle would agree to make the trip to Texas with him when he drove back home to pack. He made a mental note to talk to Brandt—hell, maybe they'd stop at the Prairie Winds Club for a couple of days on the way. He'd love to spend some time looking at Joelle's naked body spread out in the warm sunshine. It would be a treat to introduce her to the women of the Prairie Winds—damn they were a handful. Watching their Doms try to keep them corralled was some of the most fun Ryan ever had on leave.

JOELLE'S LIPS WERE still tingling from the scorching kiss Brandt had given her before heading downstairs. He'd told her to get some rest and promised to rejoin them soon. She'd watched him walk from the room, her eyes focused on his ass as her imagination wondered how long it would be until she could get her hands on those firm globes. Even though both men had been naked in the shower, they hadn't let her touch them. She hadn't protested because she'd been too tired to do much aside from trying to remain upright. Ryan's chuckle from beside her had Joelle turning to him as she felt her cheeks heat.

"Don't be embarrassed, baby. I promise you, that look

is the stuff of dreams for a Dom. I assure you Brandt would be thrilled to know you were admiring his ass—ets. But I'm sure my entire family would be grateful if you'd hold back from showing him the depth of your desire—at least for a few days. The male competition in this family is something to behold and no one wants to see Brandt's ego launched into the stratosphere." Ryan's voice was laced with nothing but affection and it warmed her heart to know how close he was with his extended family.

As an only child, she'd always envied the connection she saw between her friends and their siblings. During the past year, several of the people she'd met in Pine Creek had mentioned Brandt's struggle with PTSD and she didn't doubt for a minute Ryan was also fully aware of the hell his cousin had endured. Joelle found herself smiling at Ryan's teasing. She'd gotten to know Brandt as a friend first, so she was happy to discover his support system extended beyond his immediate family and the small community of Pine Creek.

Ryan must have sensed her mood shift because he pulled her close and pressed a kiss against her forehead. "Come on baby, let's get some sleep." She'd almost forgotten how tired she was, but the mention of rest drained the last of her second wind.

"Do you think Brandt has a t-shirt I could borrow?" When he just raised a brow in question, she quickly added, "To sleep in. I don't know what I was thinking when I packed, I completely forgot nightgowns."

"Freudian slip?" The glint in Ryan's eye told her he was only half kidding. She opened her mouth to deny his allegation, but luckily her brain kicked into gear before her mouth and she snapped it shut so quickly she felt her teeth clack together. A roguish grin lit up his face. "You know, a part of me hates the fact you caught yourself—it's likely we'd have both enjoyed your spanking." He shrugged his shoulders in a gesture she was coming to recognize as anything but nonchalant. "In time, you won't be so cognizant of your nudity."

Joelle gasped when in a move so quick she barely registered the blur, he flipped open the towel she'd wrapped around her sending it into a puddle at her feet. When she bent to retrieve it, a sharp slap heated her ass cheek making her draw in a sharp breath before dropping the damp fabric back to the floor. "Two things, baby. First of all, you don't need anything to sleep in. We're always going to want as little between us as possible. Anything you'd wear to bed will just end up shredded—so don't bother." She could tell he was trying not to laugh at her surprise. Despite her best effort, she knew her face was giving away her annoyance. Her father had often scolded her about what he called her mulish expression. She rubbed her stinging backside and watched him warily.

"Secondly, you bend over like you just did and you can be sure we're going to have our hands on you—always. And in this case, I knew you were going to wrap that towel around you blocking my view—and I wasn't interested in that at all. Now, you might want to rethink your scowl, baby, because I have to tell you that is a good way to find yourself draped over my lap. And like I said earlier, I'd be more than happy to blow off a little steam by turning those lovely cheeks of yours a lovely shade of rose."

Joelle hoped Ryan couldn't read her mind or he might decide she needed the spanking after all. She'd met Doms she would have sworn knew exactly what a sub was thinking at any given moment and it made her wonder if they weren't reading more than the body language of the woman they were topping. What Ryan didn't seem to understand was his threats to give her an over-the-knee spanking were falling on hopeful ears. The intimacy of laying over his knees with her ass bare to his palm was something she craved rather than something she feared.

Chapter Seven

RYAN WATCHED JOELLE'S expression shift from defiance to arousal in the span of a few blinks of an eye. *God in heaven, she is fucking perfect.* He hoped like hell she and Brandt would make the trip to Texas with him because he knew once he slid inside her heat, he wouldn't want to be away from her for a week. He'd been mentally cataloging her responses each time he mentioned any aspect of the lifestyle, and talking about laying her over his knee for a spanking had consistently sent her pulse and respiration rates through the roof. Her pupils dilated and the lovely pink flush of arousal moving over her chest let him know how much she loved a good spanking.

Well, never let it be said he didn't live to serve. "Brandt and I are looking forward to sharing your sweet body, but I agree—we'll need to prepare you for that pleasure." He wasn't surprised to see her eyes dilate with awareness. Joelle had probably seen several ménage scenes at the clubs where she'd played, so she knew precisely what he was talking about. He tilted his head slightly as he watched her. Damn, he'd love to know what was going through that sharp mind of hers. He could practically hear the wheels spinning furiously, her exhaustion temporarily forgotten. Oh, he knew her body was going to implode soon, all the signs were there, but he had a few minutes to play with her and the temptation was more than he could resist.

"I want you to walk over to the bed and bend at the waist. Spread your legs as far apart as you can comfortably and arch your back." The first flare of defiance he saw flash in her eyes confirmed his earlier theory—this sub needed to know her Dom would take her in hand. She was far too intelligent to blindly submit to a Dom who wasn't willing her to earn submission. "Your hesitance just earned you ten, baby. Let's go."

He shackled her small wrist with his large hand and pulled her behind him like a disobedient child to the small sitting area of Brandt's suite. This wouldn't be a harsh punishment because he knew her soul was simply giving him a glimpse of who she really was—the fact he could read her body language so perfectly made him grateful for the fact she was silently helping him far more than she knew. Ryan sat on the only armless chair but didn't pull her over his knees right away.

Using the pad of his thumb, Ryan rubbed slow, sensuous circles over the inside of her wrist. He relished the increase in her pulse as it pounded furiously beneath his touch. "Why are you being punished, baby?"

"I hesitated when you gave me an order, Sir." The slightly airy sound of her voice told him how quickly she was sliding into the scene and he could hardly wait to see the pink blush he planned to give her beautiful ass.

"Why did you hesitate?"

"I don't know. I was just trying to take everything in, and wondering how much it was going to hurt." Ryan suspected she was worried it wasn't going to hurt quite enough to get her where she needed to be—but he planned to show her how quickly he could take her exactly where she wanted to go.

"Well, I think there is a part of you that wanted this

punishment. I think you crave the intimacy you feel lying over a Dom's lap. The burn of his hand against the satin-smooth skin of her ass, his position of power as he holds you down, and the bite of pain his punishment brings—they all work together to send you into orbit, don't they, baby?"

He knew he'd nailed it when her lips parted and she sucked in a quick breath of surprise. "Yes, Sir. How did you know?" *Because your body told me, baby. You told me, even if you hadn't planned to.*

"It's Brandt's and my job to know, baby." He saw Brandt slip back into the room but knew she didn't know he'd returned. "But here's a tip for you, sweetheart. All you have to do is ask—we'll always give you what you need. And remember, one of the best parts of a polyamorous relationship would be having two men to turn to rather than just one." Shifting his gaze from her to his lap and back letting her know where she needed to be, he wanted to groan when she settled over his throbbing erection. Hell, if he made it through the next few minutes without embarrassing himself it was going to be a fucking miracle.

Once he had her in position, Brandt stepped closer and quirked an eyebrow in question. Ryan silently mouthed *hesitation* and Brandt grinned knowing that was such a subjective term a Dom could almost impose a punishment at will. Ryan had seen inexperienced Doms punish a sub for hesitation when the submissive in their care was already so far into the scene their mind was simply not processing information at their usual rate.

He slid his palm up the inside of her silky thigh until he reached the damp folds of her pussy. She wasn't dry, but she certainly wasn't dripping with arousal either—*let's see how wet you are after your paddling, sweetness.* Ryan's palm came down on her ivory skin with a resounding slap of flesh against flesh. Joelle stiffened beneath him, but she didn't even make a sound. *Interesting. Perhaps she likes the bite even more than I realized.* The first blow was followed by three more, each one just fractionally harder than the one before. He'd heard her breath hitch and the low moan when he paused letting him know he'd gotten her close to the place he wanted her. Sliding his fingers through her folds, he smiled at Brandt when his fingers came back glistening with her honey.

"Oh baby, you are enjoying this aren't you? God damn it to hell, you are fucking perfect. I can hardly wait to take this lovely ass." He kept talking while Brandt moved to the edge of the bed, laying out the lube and a couple of soft towels before stripping out of his clothes. They hadn't planned to make love to her until they'd all gotten some rest, but from the looks of his cousin, he wasn't going to get any more rest than Ryan unless he found some relief.

Four more slaps strategically placed around her pink globes and the scent of her arousal was filling the air surrounding them. God, he loved the way she smelled. He'd always loved everything about women—their sharp minds, their almost infinite capacity for love, their tender hearts, and their unfailing devotion to those they held in their hearts. Yes, women were certainly God's greatest gift to men. But this woman was beyond anything he'd ever hoped to find. Not only was she smart, but she also understood the enormous social implications of her discovery. He knew it was tearing her up to withhold the information even though it was easy to see sharing it needed to be properly staged to keep her safe. Money—or more accurately the loss of it, had a way of driving people to do horrible things to each other. Hell, even those who'd sworn their lives to the care of others could be pulled to the other side by greed.

"Your ass is the loveliest shade of rose, baby. Damn, I love that color." His fingers easily slid though her soaking folds. "Oh, sweetheart, you are so slick, so ready." Pushing his fingers into her heat, he smiled when he felt the walls of her vagina quivering around him. He pumped two fingers in and out curving them so they pressed against the soft spongy spot at the front of her channel. God, he loved the low moan coming from the back of her throat with each pass. As soon as he felt her starting to go over, he pulled his fingers free and delivered the last two swats with more force than he'd used previously, he knew the extra bit of heat was all he need to fuel her release.

Leaning down he spoke against her ear, "Come for us, Joelle." Her reaction was immediate and cataclysmic. Her scream overriding the sound of his fingers fucking her—damn, he loved those wet sounds. Knowing her body craved their touch was intoxicating. It quaked with the rolling tide as wave after wave of her orgasm swept through her. It was beautiful to watch the muscles tightening beneath her pale skin.

As the shudders slowly began to subside, Brandt lifted her from Ryan's lap and quickly positioned her face down on the bed. The pillows his cousin had placed there earlier lifted her hips in the air at the perfect angle. Granted, he'd wanted to see her lovely ass displayed over the edge of the bed, but after the release she'd just experienced he doubted she'd have been able to stand. Looking down on her as she took deep breaths trying to bring herself back down from the high, he grinned over at Ryan. *Might as well save yourself the trouble sweetheart, because we're going to send you right back up and over the mountain.*

Joelle felt her body shiver against the cotton bed covering, but not because she was cold. She'd been completely wrecked by Ryan's *punishment* because it had been anything but. What was it about these two men that made her mind and body forget they were connected? Brandt had carried her to the bed and as weak as it made her feel, she knew her legs wouldn't have held her after the orgasm she'd just experienced. There were no words to describe how eye opening the entire experience had been.

She wasn't fool enough to miss the fact her hesitation had been an excuse for Ryan to give her what he already knew she needed. But even she'd been shocked at her reaction to his punishment. She'd never completely lost herself during a scene until last night with Brandt and now she'd experienced the same intensity with Ryan. If she hadn't already been exposed to polyamorous relationships in club settings, Joelle might be freaked out about the fact she was equally attracted to two Doms. But the fact she'd seen ménage relationships work, at least in the short term, helped take the edge off her anxiety.

"Arch your back for me, minx." The rough sound of Brandt's voice brought her back to the moment, even if his words sent a small spike of fear through her. She'd never been a fan of anal play. Her one and only experience had not only been unpleasant, it had been downright painful. She'd been in college and had been overjoyed when her boyfriend asked her if she'd be interested in visiting one of the local kind clubs. A trickle of cool lubricant slid over her rear hole and Joelle felt a calloused finger massaging the sesame-scented oil into the tight right ring of muscles her boyfriend had torn so long ago. God, Joelle could still remember the humiliation she'd felt lying on the table in the club's first aid station while four virtual strangers examined her most intimate parts. It hadn't mattered three of them were medical professionals who happened to be in the club that night and the fourth was the club's owner. The humiliation Joelle experienced during the scene she'd been totally unprepared for had been totally eclipsed by the abasement she felt during their intimate examination later in the owner's office.

Joelle had been so lost in her memories she hadn't realized Brandt's fingers were no longer circling her anus in slow, soothing circles. "Where did you go, Joelle? I know this area of the body is a storehouse for memories, both good and bad. And I'm fairly certain you weren't remembering anything pleasant."

"I...well, I was just remembering the first time I tried ana....ummm...this. And, well, it didn't really go that well." She felt the bed shift as the cheeks of her ass were pulled further apart. *Oh, fucking hell, here we go again. Why didn't I just keep my damned mouth shut?*

"Were you injured, baby? Because there is evidence of tissue tearing, but I don't think the tears were treated because of the way they've healed." *Well, yippee-fucking-Skippy. Let's take pictures and use Joelle's ignorance as a warning to other unwitting subs.* Before she could close her legs and move, a large hand wrapped around the top of her thigh stilling any move she would have made. "Talk to us, baby. We don't want to hurt you—either physically or emotionally, and I think it's pretty evident someone else wasn't as cautious."

God, she wanted to bury her face in the bedding and pray for the earth to swallow her whole. She'd avoided all but the mildest forms of anal play since that night, but she'd often wondered what it would be like with someone who knew what they were doing. Having her boyfriend break up with her the next day in a text message had almost been a relief. He blamed her for his membership being revoked, but she could have told him that decision was made by the club's owner because he'd ducked out leaving her alone at the club.

Being abandoned...on top of everything else she'd endured that night had been the straw that broke the camel's back. She'd broken down in the club owner's massive office and he'd been positively livid that the man who'd hurt her had also left her to fend for herself. Up to that point, he'd been understanding and concerned, but he'd also remained all business. But evidently he was one of those men who didn't handle women's tears well because she'd almost felt the shift in him as he'd held her while she cried. From what she learned later, Master B had unleashed his rage on her ex the next morning, and even though she'd never gone back to his club, she'd always considered him her knight in shining armor.

She finally took a deep breath hoping it would help keep the anxiety she felt from showing in her voice. "My first experience wasn't good. I haven't done much anal play since. But...well, I've been curious. Curious about what everyone else is talking about." *Because all of those people in the chat rooms she'd lurked in couldn't be wrong, could they?*

Joelle wasn't able see their faces, but she knew without even turning around they were sharing a look. It amazed her how efficient their non-verbal communication seemed to be and wondered briefly if it was because they'd both been in the military. Maybe it was the fact they were cousins...or Doms. Hell, for all she knew it was all three.

Warm hands began caressing the lower curves of her ass and Joelle felt her muscles begin to relax. "What's your safe word, minx?" Joelle recited the details of the standard safe word system used in most clubs. After the disaster at Master X's club, she'd never wanted to use anything but a club safe word. Her boyfriend had managed to ignore the safe word long enough to do some serious damage because he'd thought she was being pathetically weak just to gain sympathy from the small audience gathered around them. Because the dungeon monitors hadn't known *arrête* meant stop they simply watched until one of the club's unattached submissives finally spoke up.

Joelle didn't make any effort to rein in her thoughts as Brandt worked the lube around her clenched hole with such a light touch she felt the muscles begin to slowly relax. "Good girl. I know that was hard for you, baby, but damn watching Brandt's finger pushing against your pink rosebud is hotter than hell. Let him stretch you slowly and we'll use a small plug tonight. The last thing we'd ever want to do is hurt you." Ryan words wafted over her bare back like a soft summer breeze leaving a trail of goose flesh where it teased her sensitive skin.

Joelle felt her breathing shift to short, shallow panting and she could hear the pounding of her heart. *God, it's so loud, surely they can hear it.* It seemed like hours but had to have been no more than a couple of minutes, one finger had turned to two, and then she felt the tip of something entirely different breaching her. Joelle realized she was actually pressing back into the pressure as Brandt slowly slid the tip of the plug in and out, going fractionally deeper with every stroke.

"When Brandt pushes the plug the last quarter of an inch, I want you to come for us, baby. And while you're flying over the moon, he's going to take his own pleasure." Somewhere in the back of her mind, Joelle wondered if she would be able to come again, but the thought was so fleeting she barely caught it as it flew past her consciousness. The last stoke seated the plug and Ryan's command to "Come, now" was unneeded. The instant Brandt slid his cock into her, Joelle was lost.

Every muscle in her body locked down and she felt as if she'd been launched into a colorful oblivion filled with the sound of rushing air. The brilliant bursts and streaks of color behind her eyelids were blindingly beautiful, and there was a part of her brain floating happily in appreciation for how deep the men took her into her own pleasure before sending her to heaven. The French certainly had it right when they referred to orgasm as *la petit mort*, or the "little death." Holy hat racks and hurricanes, she wasn't sure she was going to be able to hold on because darkness was encroaching from all sides at an alarming pace.

"Take a breath, Joelle." The sharp command came from Ryan. Hell, when had she turned her over? His face filled her field of vision and she wanted to do as he'd said, but nothing in her body was working right…and hell, her brain felt like it had been scrambled. "God damn it, take a breath before I have to start CPR." *CPR? Damn, I've heard that shit hurts.* Honest to God, she wanted to draw in a breath, but she couldn't make her lungs cooperate. Finally a scorching pain lashed through her breasts. She gasped a breath and realized Ryan had pinched her nipples hard enough to break through the brain fog she'd been lost in.

Sucking in huge gulps of oxygen, Joelle tried to stay focused on Ryan's violet eyes. *I wonder if he knows how beautiful he is. And where is Brandt? Why isn't he here? Did I disappoint them too? Damn, I should have known better. Master*

B said I'd be fine with a Dom who knew what he was doing, but maybe he was wrong.

Brandt's face swam in front of her, his smile looked strained and she felt tears fill her eyes. "Don't cry, minx. I'm right here. It just took me a few seconds to make my way back to Earth." He pulled her limp body into a crushing hug, rocking her back and forth before easing her away far enough he could look into her eyes. "Later we're going to want to know who Master B is—I want to thank him for taking such good care of you. But for now, I just need to hold you."

Joelle didn't fight him. Hell, she didn't have the energy to move and that was going to make fighting pretty difficult. She'd heard subs talk about experiences like this, but she'd always assumed they were exaggerating. Laughing to herself, she couldn't hold back her mental head shake…God she'd been missing out on this? *Fool!*

RYAN LEANED AGAINST the headboard of the bed holding Joelle in his arms, watching her drift in and out of sleep. Brandt had finally staggered to the bathroom and returned with a warm cloth to clean their little treasure. He'd patted her dry and then returned to the bathroom to clean himself up. Ryan's cock throbbed under Joelle despite the fact he'd come in his own hand just watching what had taken place between Brandt and the angel sleeping so peacefully in his arms. When she opened sleepy eyes and gave him a lopsided grin Ryan couldn't hold back his chuckle. "Well, hello there, sweetness. That was some ride you gave Master Brandt." Her cheeks turned scarlet in just a few heartbeats and in those few seconds Ryan had fallen helplessly in love with her.

"There is no way for me to describe how incredible it was. I'd heard other subs talk about it, but I'd never experienced anything even close to that...but..." Ryan knew exactly where this conversation was headed. There was no way she'd missed his cock pressing into the side of her hip. What she didn't know was he'd already taken the edge off—hell, and he still felt like his cock was going to split down the side the skin was stretched so tight.

He shook his head and smiled. "Let's rest a while before we start round two." He chuckled as the argument he knew hovered on her lips faded into relief. There wasn't any doubt they were all exhausted. Brandt gave him a sympathetic smile as he tugged her closer so she was sandwiched between them. He knew his cousin hadn't meant for things to get that out of control. This was supposed to be a gentle introduction to the joys of ménage, but everything about the scene had accelerated from zero to warp speed in the span of a few seconds.

As he drifted off to sleep, Ryan let his mind replay the expressions he'd seen move over Joelle's face during her spanking. He was sure she hadn't noticed the mirror on the other side of the room, but it had provided him with a perfect view of her changing expressions as he'd meted out her punishment. He couldn't wait to push himself as deep as possible into her softness. He was going to push Doc Slow to wind things up as quickly as possible tomorrow because he was anxious to spend some quality time with Joelle—preferably naked, before hitting the road.

Now he wasn't going to take no for an answer, she and Brandt would make the trip with him or he would hire movers and be done with it. It wasn't that he needed the help, he'd just wanted the three of them to have a few days to spend together while the security teams he and Brandt had enlisted figured out who was targeting Joelle. Neither he nor Brandt had asked her where she'd hidden the formula—hell, he didn't really want to know. Anyone smart enough to make what would probably be hailed as one of the biggest medical breakthroughs of the century was certainly smart enough to guard the information carefully.

Chapter Eight

HELEN RODRICK THREW her phone across the room satisfied when the offending device exploded into a hundred pieces from the impact. Her assistant would have a new one on her desk within the hour. The damn man must buy them by the case, but then she did have a habit of destroying them whenever her caller failed to provide whatever news she wanted. *How could they have lost her? And now she is staying in a place that might as well be fucking Fort Knox?* The incompetence of help these days was something to behold.

How one woman could be so difficult to contain was absolutely baffling. Hell, entire countries had been brought to heel in less time. Not only had the boobs she'd hired failed to secure the information she'd requested, but they'd managed to lose the woman, too. Helen agreed she was likely headed to Texas with Dr. Ryan Morgan and Sheriff Brandt Morgan since they'd all three left the small mountain town at the same time. But, God damn it, there was a lot of space between those two places. There were literally thousands of miles of highways between Montana and Texas, searching for them now was like trying to find the proverbial needle in a haystack.

But on the bright side…Joelle Phillips was running scared, which meant she wouldn't be going public with the damned formula anytime soon. The election was just a few months away, if she could hold out until then, her options would expand exponentially. Taking a calming breath, she turned to her desk to call her assistant about her phone. Helen gasped in surprise when she saw him standing in front of her desk holding a new phone. "Ready to go, Ms. Rodrick. If there's nothing else, I'll be leaving for the day." She nodded and watched as he walked from the room.

The debris from her earlier lapse in control had already been removed and once again she wondered if her right hand man wasn't a fucking ninja. Firing off one last text, she smiled and made her way out the door. Since both men had been Navy SEALS, it made sense they'd choose the most efficient route to Dr. Morgan's family compound in Houston…unless they decided to visit friends along the way. Knowing who their contacts were would go a long way to predicting their route. And God knew they'd be far more vulnerable away from either family home—*Jesus, what's with those people anyway. Security out the ass…hell you'd think they were paranoid or something.* Laughing at her own absurdity, she pushed all the unpleasantness out of her mind and headed out the door.

TOBI WEST FIDGETED on the bar stool as she looked out over the early arrivals for Friday night fun and kinky games at the Prairie Winds Club. Her best friend, Gracie, sat serenely next to her sipping on a soda and looking as calm as Tobi was wired. Their children were gone for the week…a blessing from God in the form of a grandparents' trip to Florida. Tobi's husbands hadn't been thrilled to let their darling children leave, but she'd danced around the room for an hour…and that was just when it had been first mentioned. She'd been over the moon thinking about all the downtime she and Gracie were going to enjoy without their darling demons underfoot.

"Sit still. Your Masters are going to think you're scheming, and I'll be presumed guilty by association. And, I don't want to start off this week with my buns toasted because you won't flipping SIT STILL." *Damn, lighten up already, bestie.*

"Geez. Alright already. Keep your shirt…umm…bustier on why don't you? No need to get all pissy." Tobi tried to act contrite but she was pretty sure it hadn't played well when Gracie rolled her eyes.

"What do you know about the company rolling in tonight? I haven't been able to get much out of Micah or Jax, which could mean they are friends from the military or people who know a friend…who knows a guy from college…who is a neighbor to Cousin Barney, who once had a cat that visited a neighbor they got to know." Tobi had just taken a drink of her lemonade and spewed it in a fine mist all over the floor in front of her. Thank God no one had been walking by, she'd have already been in trouble. She'd only been there five minutes and that might be a record even for her. *No, the time you got busted walking through the main lounge carrying your tablet still holds the record.* Damn it to hell, she hated the security cameras that seemed to be programmed to tract her every move.

"I didn't get much from Kent or Kyle either. Just that the guys are former SEALs and the woman is theirs." She said the last word with air quotes because her husbands had both emphasized the point making her wonder what they thought she was going to do, hit on the woman or something? Geez. Not that she cared what others did, but Tobi really couldn't see it ever happening. Hell, who needed another man or woman when she had Kent and Kyle West in her bed?

"All I know is the men want to spend time together trying to work out some threat to Joelle...that's her name by the way."

"Threat? What kind of threat?" Tobi went on point immediately. She was by nature inquisitive...her husbands called her a snoop, but she was sticking with curious because it sounded much better. She'd been a reporter before marrying the West brothers and was still very capable of putting a nice *spin* on a story, thank you very much.

"I don't really know. When I started to ask last night, my men pulled the old distract her with sex routine."

"Yeah, I know that one well. And just FYI, the silly grin on your face tells me how well their tag teaming worked. Damn, girl, your game face needs work."

"Tobi," Kent's stern voice came from right behind her causing her to squeak in surprise. *Thank God it wasn't Kyle*. Kent was far more open-minded about her cursing, whereas Kyle was completely obsessed with striking those words from her vocabulary. *Not fucking likely*.

"Sorry, sir." She glared at Gracie, who was grinning at her like a loon—oh yeah, her friend had known he was standing behind her alright. "And your loyalty could use a re-charge as well, *bestie*." The words hadn't been spoken with any real heat so Gracie would know she wasn't in so deep a dozen or so chocolate chip cookies wouldn't bail her out.

Kent slid his arm around her, his fingers immediately tunneling under the edge of her halter-top to cup her breast. Pinching her nipple between two fingers and then rolling it back and forth in a motion so slow Tobi knew he was deliberately teasing her. She tried to ignore his torturing touch, but he was playing her like a finely tuned instrument. *Damn it, he knows more about my body than I do. It's just not fair.* When Gracie snorted a laugh, Tobi wanted to groan in frustration. She'd spent so much time alone as a child she'd learned to talk to herself to break the tedium of oppressive silence...and it was a habit she still struggled to break.

"I do indeed know your body better than you do because I pay very close attention, sweetness. I'm paying very good attention right now because I can feel your body winding up perfectly. If I slid my hand between those lovely thighs of yours would my fingers come back coated with your honey?" *Damn and double damn. He knew exactly what he was doing to her. Wet? Try soaked. Drenched? Sopping? Dripping?* Oh hell, there had to be more words to use, but the dual sensation of her nipple being rolled between his fingers and the sting as he bit down on the top of her shoulder was scrambling her brain.

Tobi tilted her head to the side and moaned as a bolt of heat traveled from her nipple straight to her pussy. "Kitten, I believe your Master asked you a question." Tobi hadn't even realized she'd closed her eyes, but letting her lashes flutter open she wasn't surprised to see Kyle sitting in the seat where Gracie had been moments earlier. He had a way of drifting in as silent as smoke. She credited his ability to slip up on her silently on his mad ninja skills and damn if those secret super hero abilities didn't get her into a lot of trouble sometimes.

"She doesn't seem to be very focused this evening. Maybe we should make her come right here. A nice screaming orgasm ought to set the tone for the evening, don't you think?" Kent was teasing...at least, she hoped he was teasing. She was on board with the screaming orgasm part of his proposal, but she didn't particularly want to have it in the middle of the bar. But she certainly wasn't going to admit it to either of her Doms. She'd learned very early on, admitting reluctance was the quickest way to get them to do exactly what she *didn't* want them to do. They claimed it was all about pushing her boundaries as a submissive—that was piddle and they all knew it. It was about torturing her—plain and simple.

"Well, I have to admit, I'm impressed with *piddle*, that's pretty tame compared to the sewage that often comes from between those beautiful lips. But, she still hasn't answered your question, so I think I'll up the stakes a bit."

He bit back a grin when she groaned softly, "Stakes? Up? Oh shit. What was the frick-fracking question anyway?"

"Lean her back, I think I'll just check for myself if she's ready." Kyle would have been worried she'd be able to see the amusement in his expression, but her eyes were so glazed he doubted she was seeing anything.

Kent pulled her back against his chest putting her enough off balance she had to grasp his forearms to keep from falling off the stool. She probably should have thanked him because otherwise her hands would have instinctively tried to pull her micro-ridiculously-short skirt back down. But fate played a role in her rescue as well, just as Kyle's fingers slid between her wet folds Kent spoke up, "Going to need to table this for a while. Our guests just walked in the door." Tobi was already panting, evidence of her desire already embarrassingly obvious on Kyle's fingers, and for a few seconds, she wasn't sure whether to be grateful or furious she'd been given a reprieve.

When she suddenly found herself on her feet, Tobi

swayed—no doubt the blood that was supposed to be feeding her brain had decided to head south. Kyle stepped forward motioning the three people standing at the door to join them while Kent steadied her. "Sweetness, are you okay? This timing sucks—sorry we wound you up and then had to leave you hanging." His sweet apology went a long way to calm the jitters she suddenly felt shaking their way up from her core. Damn, she'd wanted that orgasm even if she hadn't been particularly thrilled with the location. But, turns out having a scream the walls down release sitting at the club's bar was better than not having one at all. *Damn and double damn.*

JOELLE LOOKED AROUND the enormous main room of the Prairie Winds Club and couldn't hold back her smile. The place was huge and the decorations were perfect for the Hill Country of Texas. She saw several stage areas and a good-sized dance floor, but the feature that caught her eye was the metal spiral staircase. The cutouts along the side depicted various western scenes and the entire piece was nothing short of spectacular. Before she could take in everything around her, she was being led to what looked like a bar right out of...damn, what was that show?

Ryan leaned close to speak to her and she could hear the amusement in his voice. "I can see the question in your eyes—yes, the bar was fashioned to resemble Miss Kitty's in *Gunsmoke*. This might not be Dodge City, but the West brothers didn't seem to care if they were borrowing facts." Joelle listened as introductions were made, but it was the tiny blonde bombshell standing between the West brothers who captured her attention. Tobi West had an almost pained expression on her pretty face Joelle recognized all too well. *Damn, we interrupted something.*

Tobi still hadn't pulled herself together when a pretty Latino woman stepped up beside her. The men introduced her to Gracie McDonald and one of her husbands, Jax McDonald. Jax took one look at Tobi and laughed. "Damn, sweet cheeks, did your Masters wind you up and leave you floating in the breeze again?" Joelle had to swallow her giggle when Tobi growled at him. The sterner of Tobi's husbands warned her about her surly behavior but it didn't seem to bother the petite blonde much.

Gracie stood on her tiptoes to whisper in Jax's ear and he turned stroking the side of her face in a move so filled with affection Joelle found herself staring at them. "Yes, carinõ, I think that's an excellent idea. But stay in the lit areas, you know your other Master is in the control room, don't give him a reason to call me." *Control room? Oh my, what kind of place is this?* The women grabbed drinks, making sure Joelle got something as well before leading her out the back door.

"Oh my God. This is spectacular." Joelle couldn't hold back her surprise. The landscaping alone looked like something out of a movie. She read the sign directing people to the Forum Shops which Tobi explained catered to all things "kinky" including everything from the most extreme fet-wear to piercing and waxing services. They settled into comfortable lounge chairs in an open area overlooking the broad expanse of the West's backyard. "Is that a lake?" Darkness was quickly blocking out the view, but she was sure she'd seen the sparkle of lights dancing over the surface of the water.

"It's a river, but right here it's actually pretty wide so I can see why you might wonder. I wish we could go down to the gazebo, but there aren't as many cameras there and I know Micah would call Jax and tattle on us."

Gracie shook her head. "Don't start Tobi, I've already told you, I don't want to spend the whole week with a sore bum."

"Bum? Good Lord of the Leprechauns, you're turning into a pansy-assed good girl...I'll bet you're even wearing panties." When Gracie laughed, Tobi continued, "That's it, I'm going to have to get myself a new bestie. Hanging out with you will destroy my reputation...and holy crap on a cannonball, what if it's contagious? Damn it to donuts, I'll probably have nightmares about this now. Thanks for nothing Miss Goody-Two-Shoes." Tobi let out a dramatic sigh that probably would have earned her an Oscar nomination in a different venue. Holy shit could the girl ever put on a performance. And Gracie's look of righteous indignation just added to the comedic moment. Joelle couldn't hold it in a moment longer...she burst out laughing.

Damn if felt good to laugh so hard the tension of the past few days finally drained away. Joelle leaned back letting the strain she'd been under fall away. "Holy hell, you two are good for the soul...has anyone ever told you that? You make me miss my friend Coral even more. She's been my sounding board for months and now she's off bouncing around tropical islands enjoying her honeymoon."

"Coral Williams? Oh, I guess she is Coral Morgan now, isn't she?" When Joelle nodded, Tobi's face lit up. "I talked to her via web-cam. She seems really sweet, but I think there is a firecracker under there you're going to see bubble right up to the surface now that she's safe." Turning to Gracie, she added, "Remember me telling you about all the drama in Montana? Holy..." Tobi's eyes tracked around them and her voice lowered, "shiatzus, their surprise sniper was even older than Lilly." Gracie's eyes widened and her mouth formed an *oh* making Joelle wonder who Lilly was and about the story they both seemed to know.

Unable to hold back her curiosity, Joelle inquired, "Who is Lilly?"

"My audacious mother-in-law, she's my super hero."

"She's everybody's super hero." Gracie's agreement made Joelle even more curious. "Lilly saved Tobi by taking out a boat and the bad guys in it with a single rifle shot. The men swear it was luck, but I'm not buying it."

"It's a long story, but the short version is, the ass...embled hats in the boat were speeding toward me and Lilly shot into the cluster of fuel cans on the back deck by the motor. And, as Kodi would say, it was a *big boom*."

"I'm telling you, Tobi, that girl's love of explosives is going to be trouble one of these days, you just wait and see." Gracie's words were tempered by a grin that lit up her entire face. Joelle suddenly realized how much she was enjoying her time with these two women.

"Oh, please. Like she'll be able to get away with anything with so many former Special Forces guys watching her every move? Cripes, the poor girl probably won't have a date until she's thirty. Fathers, godfathers, coaches, and pals—the kid is surrounded. Personally, I think Kameron is the one everybody should be worried about...still waters run deep, you know. He is quiet, but he doesn't miss anything and he's freaking scary smart." Oh, this was something Joelle could certainly relate to, she'd heard the same thing said about herself as a child and knew exactly what sorts of things the West's young son was dreaming up.

"Well, I can tell you, I heard people express similar concerns to my father about me, and well...with good reason. I don't know how old he is, but you might refrain from buying him a science set until he's...oh, twenty-two or three...just FYI." Both women were staring at her, their mouths gaping open in shock before they simultaneously burst into fits of giggles.

"Holy ship-wreck, we're going to be great friends. That's flipping perfect and I know full well it's on tape, so I've got proof. I've been telling Kent and Kyle the same thing for months and they are so sure their sweet son is a candidate for sainthood. It amazes me they are so clueless where he is concerned." Tobi was wiping tears from her eyes she'd laughed so hard and Joelle realized she was laughing right along with them. Good heavens, what would it be like to have this woman's power to spread joy so easily? She could barely imagine.

"I love my godson with all my heart, but I'm with Tobi on this one. That boy is going to be a wild one and what worries me is he and his grandmother seem to be cut from the same cloth. If she trains him, we're all in for it. I love her, but she skates on the edge of crazy more often than not." Gracie's eyes glittered with mischief and Joelle decided Tobi's assessment of her friend as a good-girl was probably unsubstantiated.

"Okay, enough of this. Let's get to the new gossip. What's up with you, girlfriend, and who wants to take you out?"

"Tobi! Dang, you're about as subtle as a Mack truck loaded with C4." Gracie rolled her eyes at her friend then turned to Joelle. "All of the women at Prairie Winds have had stalkers in one form or another, it seems to be our group's claim to fame. So we naturally assumed you were having the same sort of problem when your guys called the Prairie Winds team in."

"Well, I'm not sure how much I'm supposed to share, but at this point, it probably isn't that big a deal."

"Despite the way it looks, we're actually really good with secrets. It's one of those *we subs have to stick together* things. We don't rat out fellow subs unless their lives are in danger. But it's your call how much you share, we're just here to lend an ear." Everything about Tobi West spoke to her sincerity. It was easy to see why she was so well liked in the kink community. Joelle had heard a lot about her over the past couple of years. She and Gracie had been busy setting up various versions of their Forum Shops in other clubs around the country and from what Joelle understood their consulting business was making money hand over fist.

Joelle quickly outlined her situation watching as their expressions changed from interest to compassion to respect and then finally worry. "Holy crapamolie, new pal of mine, I don't know whether to build a shrine to you or drop you in a bulletproof bubble and hide you." Tobi's comment made Joelle smile and that's something she hadn't been able to do before when she discussed her situation.

"I agree with Tobi, but I have to say I am so very impressed. Joelle, I'm going to enjoy telling everyone I count you among my friends. You're going to change the world in a very significant way. Everything else aside, I want you to know how proud I am to know you." Joelle's eyes filled with tears at Gracie's sincerity. Damn, she hated crying and crying when someone said something nice to you, it usually made them uncomfortable, too.

Gracie and Tobi moved to her sides wrapping their

arms around her in a show of support and friendship Joelle rarely experienced before meeting Coral a year ago. "Thanks. I admit I'm scared. The list of suspects is made up of very powerful people, but even more because I don't want anyone being hurt because they're close me. The individuals on the suspect list wouldn't think twice about what they'd see as collateral damage."

"Yeah, the irony of people getting hurt trying to prevent something that will save so many lives is pretty hard to miss. Cheese and crackers, people amaze me. I've been poor, so I understand all the opportunities money offers…but I can't imagine any situation where I would put money over the life of even one innocent person." For the first time, Joelle saw another side of Tobi's personality. This was a woman who loved those around her fiercely and who came to the defense of those who couldn't fight for themselves. With her next breath, Joelle realized it was exactly who she wanted to be. It was damned humbling to realize she'd been letting fear keep her from doing what was *right*.

She stood up ready to make her way back inside. She'd needed to find Brandt and Ryan; it was time to ask them to help her make her discovery public. It might take two or three years before the treatment was readily available, but at the very least she needed to make sure the world knew hope was on the way. When she turned to the path they'd used earlier, she came face-to-face with Ryan. His smile was indulgent, but his eyes stared straight into the depths of her soul. Quirking a brow, he asked, "Going somewhere, baby?"

"Yes. I was coming to find you and Brandt. I need to talk to you. I need to do something. I've wasted too much time being scared." All the words tumbled out so quickly she wondered if he'd be able to sort it all through. His smile softened and he brushed his fingers down the side of her face in a caress so gentle she knew it was a prelude to whatever he was going to say.

"Brilliant and brave—damn, you are an amazing combination." He didn't say anything else but stepped aside as Tobi and Gracie both excused themselves with promises to meet again later in the evening.

"You already knew, didn't you? You knew I'd decided." She wasn't sure whether to be annoyed or grateful Ryan and Brandt always seemed to know what she was thinking—often before she even realized where her thoughts were headed.

"No. But when Micah alerted me to the conversation you were having with Tobi and Gracie, it wasn't a stretch to know where it would lead you." He grinned and pressed a soft kiss to her forehead. "Tobi West has an amazing effect on everyone she meets. She's a handful—don't get me wrong, I know she leads her husbands on a merry chase and they adore her for it. But her joy and compassion shine through from the very depths of her soul, and it draws out the best in those around her. I'd only met her a couple of times before this trip, but from what I'd heard, I'm not surprised your conversation led to this. Truthfully, your time with them wasn't an accident. Everyone working on this case believed the two of them might be a good sounding board for you since Coral isn't available. What's that old saying? Something about girlfriends and sisters being better than therapists?"

Joelle wasn't sure how she felt about Ryan inferring she needed a therapist, but she understood what he'd meant. Without giving herself a chance to hesitate, she threw her arms around him hugging him close. At that moment, with his arms wrapped tightly around her, everything seemed so simple. The decision seemed easy and the sea ahead smooth sailing. She knew reality was going to be far different, but she wanted to enjoy the illusion for a little while. Reality could wait…at least until tomorrow.

Chapter Nine

RYAN AND BRANDT had already enlisted the help of every resource they thought might be even remotely helpful in their attempt to uncover who was responsible for the problems Joelle had been facing. The Wests and their team were also working to narrow down the list of suspects, but so far had only eliminated a couple of people from the list Joelle had given them.

The consensus of the team members meeting in Kyle and Kent's office was Joelle was probably right, former senator Helen Rodrick was the most likely suspect. Her obvious ties to two different pharmaceuticals companies, and the hidden ties they'd uncovered to several other companies, that would take a huge financial hit when the news of her discovery broke put her at the top of their list. Adding all that to the fact the woman was running for President made her not only their prime suspect but also a frighteningly powerful adversary. Hell, even eluding to such a suspicion would put them on the watch list of every alphabet agency in the damned country—not something agents involved in covert ops for the government could afford.

While the other men made some discrete calls inquiring about Ms. Roderick's known associates and employees, Ryan had drawn the prized straw and gotten distraction duty. Christ, how lucky was he to be the one who got to entertain the gorgeous redhead who'd just had the revelation they'd all been expecting. Kent West had called it right when he'd said a short conversation with Tobi would drive anyone to an epiphany.

The only call Ryan made before coming to find Joelle was a brief conference call with his dad and uncle. Brothers Donald and Dean Morgan had remained close despite choosing vastly different career paths. Geographically they'd settled miles apart, but both men had a Midas touch when it came to business. From all accounts, Dean's eldest son, Sage, had inherited his father's and uncle's same business acumen. There had been talk recently of combining Morgan Enterprises and Morgan Energy so Dean and Donald could retire, making Sage the CEO of the newly formed Morgan Holdings. Ryan had encouraged the plan; with the stipulation the combined company also branch out into medical research. And now, after finding Joelle, his support of that joint venture was going to be even more adamant.

The elder Morgan brothers were putting their heads together to organize a press conference in Houston for Joelle to share her discovery with the world. Their media connections would go a long way to ensuring Joelle's safety. The best way to dodge a bullet was to put several things between the sniper and the target. She'd been on her own long enough, it was time to show her what family support was all about. Her father may love her in his own skewed way, but from what Ryan had learned over the past few days, the man hadn't backed her when it mattered the most. There was a part of him that resented the hell out of the way she'd been treated. What could she accomplish if she had the kind of family support he and Brandt had been privileged to grow up with? Hell, their family still had their backs—it was the way things were supposed to work.

Holding Joelle in his arms soothed him in a way nothing else ever had. It was a good thing he hadn't known she'd have this effect on him when they first met—hell, he'd have probably never finished med-school. Her spine had been ramrod straight when he'd first pulled her against him, but after a few seconds, she'd relaxed into his arms. Feeling the tension drain from her body as she made the decision to let him lead her where she needed to go pumped up his ego to what his friends would probably feel was a dangerous degree—but he didn't care.

"As much as I'm enjoying this moment and as fulfilling as I find it to just hold you in my arms, we need to head inside—I have something special planned for you."

Joelle lifted her face giving him an uncertain smile. "A surprise? Remember, I'm a scientist, so surprises aren't really my forte." It was obvious she was choosing her words carefully though he wasn't sure who she was trying to appease—herself or him.

Deciding this was a good time to clear up that particular point, he cupped his hands around both sides of her face smoothing feathered strokes over her flushed cheeks. "Baby, don't ever feel like you need to measure your words around me. I won't presume to speak for Brandt, but I can tell you my experience has been he won't want you to feel as if you need to always be on guard. We'll demand your honesty—not only with us but also with yourself, that is nonnegotiable. There will be times we don't *like* what you have to say, but as long as you aren't rude, we'll respect your right to express your opinion."

She nodded in understanding and Ryan couldn't wait to get back inside so he let the non-verbal answer go unchallenged. "Now, remember, even though I'm not a stickler for high protocol, this is a kink club and as you know there are basic rules universal between clubs regardless of where they're located. Keep those in mind when we cross the threshold because the last thing I want to waste time on is dealing with some damned self-professed super Dom who wants to lay his hands on what Brandt and I consider ours." He hoped his grin would ease some of the anxiety he knew his words would likely instill once she took a deep breath and considered what he'd said. The declaration had been necessary, but it didn't mean it wouldn't be unsettling.

"Yours?" *Well, that didn't take long.* Ryan wasn't sure what part she hadn't understood or if she was simply denying their claim on her.

"Yes, ours. If that's a problem for you, I suggest you speak up before this goes any further." There was a bite to his tone, but Ryan didn't care—this needed to be cleared up quickly. He studied her closely—hell, he was watching her so closely he saw the subtle shift in her eyes and the small creases at the corners seem to recede as her cheeks flushed.

"Really?" This time, the question was more hopeful than questioning and Ryan let out a breath he hadn't realized he was holding.

"Yes, really. Christ woman, I can see why Brandt calls you minx." Pulling her hand, he led her back to the open doors of the club's main room. He'd set up one of the small stages near the back where they wouldn't attract as much attention and he couldn't wait to get started. Hopefully, Brandt would be joining them before the scene was over, but he had every intention of keeping her fully focused on their scene instead of worrying about why her other Master was missing.

Leading her up the three steps and to the center of the small stage, he saw her eyes widen at the odd-looking apparatus in front of her. It was a very specialized version of a St. Andrew's Cross—one the West brothers had specially built and modified it a time or two over the past couple of years. The cuffs were extra-wide and lined with removable fabric pads that were changed after each use so they were not only comfortable, but also sanitary—an important perk as far as Ryan was concerned.

The cross was made of metal finished to look like an antique relic from the old west, but the state of the art lighting and hydraulic systems definitely made it a Dom's best friend. There wasn't any part of a submissive a Dom couldn't secure or expose for his pleasure using this amazing piece of equipment, and the options for positioning his or her body were unlimited.

Ryan gave Joelle several seconds to take in everything around her before stepping closer and bringing her attention back to him. He could see her pulse pounding rapidly at the base of her throat. Her breathing had become faster, shallower with every breath she took. And her eyes were dilated with what appeared to be a healthy mix of arousal and anxious anticipation. *Perfect*.

"Strip, baby. I want access to every luscious inch of you and I want everyone in this club to see what lucky bastards Brandt and I are." She took a deep breath and slowly gathered the hem of the short black dress they'd chosen for her. Joelle crushed the hem in her fists before pulling it over her head in a move so inherently seductive he wondered for a few seconds if she was deliberately taunting him. The garment they'd given her was obscenely short and cut to her navel, hell it was little more than a piece of black silk. Of course, they'd conveniently forgotten her panties so in one deliberate move she was standing in front of him completely bare.

Swirling the tip of his finger around the outer edge of her deep pink areola of first one breast and then the other, Ryan watched with satisfaction as her nipples pebbled so tightly he knew they had to be aching with need. "Perfection. You are pure perfection, love. Every time I look at you, I'm amazed anyone can be so beautiful both inside and out." He'd kept his voice pitched low to enhance the intimacy between them—he wanted her focused on him, not their growing audience.

Trailing his fingers along an imaginary line between her rounded breasts he traced a leisurely path all the way to her navel. Leaning down, he swirled the tip of his tongue around the outer edge before tickling the center with several quick lashes. "You always taste like fire and honey. Sweet, yet scorching hot. You're an addiction I don't ever want to be overcome. I'll treasure each moment together and cherish your trust every single day."

She was already falling so far into the submissive mindset he wasn't sure she fully comprehended what he was telling her, but he'd keep telling her until she understood. He and Brandt agreed her childhood had left her feeling as though she had little value aside from academics. From everything they'd learned, her father had loved her in his own way, but the rare displays of affection had always been tied to some accomplishment. For a young girl with a submissive mindset it hadn't taken her long to associate approval with academic achievement—now it was their job to teach the woman she'd become the joys of unconditional love.

Using the pads of his fingers, Ryan drew lazy circles over her bare mons. God, he loved being able to see every inch of her. He'd almost swallowed his tongue when he learned all the smooth skin hadn't come from waxing but was a result of a rare personal indulgence. Joelle blushed when she told them how she'd gone to the spa with her college roommate. And after just one waxing decided she loved the look and feel of the results, but she hadn't been able to imagine repeating the experience every three months so she'd researched options. *Always the researcher.* She'd opted for laser treatments, deciding the temporary discomfort once was far better than repeating the experience several times a year. Personally, Ryan was thrilled—the thought of anyone other than he or Ryan having their hands so close to sex made him see red.

"Slide your feel further apart, baby. I want access to those slick folds. I want to be able to fuck you with my fingers and feel your muscles clamping tight as they try to pull me deeper inside." Her feet slid apart and her eyelids slid lower as she fell further and further into the scene. It only took a few pumps of his fingers to bring her right to the edge of release, but he had no intention of letting her come so quickly.

When he pulled his fingers free, she groaned at the loss and a shudder worked through her when he licked his fingers clean. The sweet honey still coated his tongue when he leaned forward and kissed her. The kiss he'd meant to be sweet and tempting—a little sample of her taste, turned carnal and incendiary almost from the beginning. Ryan slid his other hand up the straight line of her spine to tunnel under her long, silky red hair. Cupping the base of her skull, Ryan tilted her head allowing him to deepen the kiss. Thrusting his tongue into her mouth with long, strong strokes mimicking the move his dick longed to repeat, he felt her beginning to go lax in his hold. Stepping back, he moved her quickly into place in front of the cross and secured her before he lost his damned mind completely and fucked her right where they stood.

Pulling a hair clip from his back pocket, Ryan twisted the silky length of her hair into a rope before securing it against the back of her head with the turquoise clip. Leaning over her shoulder, he spoke against her ear, "I wanted your beautiful hair off your back so it doesn't get tangled in the braided lashes of the flogger, baby." Opening his mouth over the sensitive spot where her neck joined her shoulder, Ryan clamped down until she gasped softly. That sweet sound sent a bolt of electricity straight to his cock. Christ, he was already worried about a permanent zipper imprint and now he felt himself swelling enough he worried he would burst.

"I'm going to warm you up, baby. And then I'm going to send you so far up you'll wonder if the pleasure is ever going to end. But rest assured, love—Master Brandt and I will *always* catch you, so don't hesitate to take flight when you're given permission." Stepping back, he began the slow, methodical thuds against the fleshiest parts of her ass. Her skin was so fair the soft lashes brought the blood to the surface and quickly turning her ivory skin a spectacular shade of rosy-pink. As he spread out the falls, he slowly increased the pace but not the intensity of the strikes so she'd sink as far into the sensations as possible before the balance of pleasure and pain started to tip ever so slightly in the other direction.

BRANDT HAD BEEN totally enthralled as he watched Joelle and Ryan's scene. Every security feed in the control room had a joystick allowing whoever was manning the station to zoom in—the video so crystal clear he'd been able to hear every breathless sigh and see each and every goose-pebbled inch of alabaster skin as he'd finished up his calls. It was a miracle he hadn't broken his damned neck racing down the fucking spiral staircase to get to there. And now, standing at the edge of the small stage, watching Ryan send her so deep into subspace her entire body was vibrating to what he suspected was an internal rhythm much like the constant beating of the ocean waves against the shore. She was safely secured to the West's modified cross so there was no worry she'd injure herself. He was grateful because she was obviously falling helplessly over the edge of what was going to be a cataclysmic release. He doubted either of them were aware of the increasing volume of the audience as the other Doms used the moment to bring their own submissives pleasure.

Brandt understood why the other club members were so captivated with the scene—hell, it was beyond hot. What amazed him was how unaware Ryan seemed to be of his surroundings. The man had been a Navy SEAL for fuck's sake. Dom-space was a great place to be, but it could be dangerous. The scene was taking place in a BDSM club, so there was a lot of support close by, but this clearly illustrated why it was always advisable to play in a club or with a third person nearby. When both Dom and sub were this focused, they were both far too vulnerable.

He felt Kyle West step up beside him before he actually saw him. Kyle had always exuded the kind of presence associated with leaders and alpha males—he was one of the few men Brandt had ever known who could walk down the crowded streets of Hong Kong without so much as a single physical encounter. No one jostled Kyle West. Hell, people unconsciously cleared a path for him to walk unobstructed through markets that were a labyrinth of humanity others had to weave through. Tobi was the only person Brandt had ever seen stand up to Kyle—aside from his twin brother, of course.

Brandt remembered hearing about Tobi and Kyle's first meeting. She'd been on her way to interview Kent for some local magazine, but her car hydroplaned off the highway during a thunderstorm leaving her stranded along the side of the road. After several unsuccessful attempts to stop a passing motorist, she'd stood in the middle of the highway so she wouldn't be missed by the next vehicle driving by. Kyle had nearly hit the petite blonde bundle of trouble. When he'd stopped and made his way back to her, he'd been furious. His anger fueled by fear at the close call and adrenaline drenched relief she was unharmed. But she'd stood toe-to-toe with him, despite the fact Kyle was easily a foot taller, refusing to back down as he'd questioned her intelligence and sanity.

The night Kyle shared the story with him, Brandt had struggled to keep from laughing at the mental picture flashing through his mind. But after meeting Tobi, Brandt didn't have any trouble imagining her fire, and it was obvious to everyone who knew Kyle, she'd been exactly what he'd needed. While Kent had always been far more flexible and easy-going in general, Kyle had been well on his way to becoming isolated by his own rules. Brandt knew Tobi had won the hearts of Kyle's friends and family for that alone.

"They don't know there is anyone else in the room, do they?" Kyle's whispered words brought Brandt back to the moment. "Tobi can do that to Kent—it's one of the things I envy about my brother, his ability to soar in Dom space."

"I was just thinking the same thing. I've never seen Ryan completely lost in a scene before."

"And you're worried about their safety." It hadn't been a question, Kyle had already known what Brandt was thinking. "He knew he was safe here. As a matter of fact, Ryan went to a lot of trouble to ensure their safety ahead of time. If you take a look around, you'll see several men stationed around the area who aren't focused on the scene—they're watching exits and the audience for anything even remotely threatening."

Brandt felt as if a huge burden had been lifted from his shoulders. He hadn't even realized how worried he'd been until he saw how much care Ryan had taken to ensure Joelle's safety. "I know it might seem like over-kill on my part, but she is incredibly special. And I don't mean she is only special to us—hell, her discovery is going to make a huge difference in the world someday. I think we all know it will be years before the full effects are felt, but the ripples will start the minute she drops the pebble in the pond."

"I agree. I believe my dads are getting involved in the process as well. They're coordinating with your dad and uncle to make sure Joelle's announcement is heard round the world." Brandt turned to him, curious about the note of amusement he heard in Kyle's voice. "I think they are trying very hard to keep Mom from *helping*. She has a way of attracting trouble, much like the little mischief magnet I'm married to. I'm just grateful they are still in Florida. Hopefully, that's far enough." Brandt heard the worry in Kyle's voice and had to fight back his laugh. *Hell, with Lilly West, the width of the Gulf of Mexico might not be enough distance.*

He stifled the laughter threatening to break free because saying Lilly West attracted trouble was one hell of an understatement. The last Brandt knew, she was on Homeland Security's "avoid if at all possible" list. When she'd found out Brandt was a sniper, she begged him to teach her how to shoot one of his preferred rifles. Her husbands and sons had been horrified and threatened him with great bodily harm if he did any such thing. To this day, she still asked every time he saw her if he'd changed his mind. From what Brandt could see, Tobi was well on her way to becoming the next Lilly West—or worse.

Chapter Ten

JOELLE TRIED TO bring the world into focus, but the only thing she knew for certain was she was warm and safe. Trying to sort through the source of her confusion felt like swimming in a pool filled with chocolate pudding. The more she strained to see past the goo, the more confused she became. Finally giving in to the lure of sleep, Joelle let the stinging skin on her back and ass warm her so sleep could easily pull her under. There would be time to figure out what happened later, for now, she was going to relish the sweet oblivion of slumber.

RYAN WAS DAMNED glad Brandt was the one carrying Joelle up the spiral staircase because he wasn't sure he would have trusted his legs to carry such precious cargo up the curving metal stairs. Hell, he wasn't entirely convinced they were going to carry *him* up the stairs. The scene with Joelle had blown apart everything he thought he'd known about topping a sub. He'd known from the outset it was going to be intense but it exceeded his wildest expectations. From the moment he'd told her to strip, Joelle had shifted all of her focus to him.

He wasn't sure he'd ever seen a sub fall into subspace so quickly or so completely. He and Brandt would have to remember to always secure her safely before beginning a scene. Ryan wondered briefly how she would respond to shibari. Even though he was out of practice, he couldn't help wondering what she would look like bound in the decorative rope designs showcasing her for their erotic pleasure. He'd studied the ancient Japanese bondage technique years ago because he'd felt drawn to the artistic expression of eroticism. The two elements were simply different sides of the same coin. Sex was, by nature, frenzied and messy, but the artistry of shibari required time and patience; and it showcased not only the subject's trust in the artist, but it displayed his or her body as well.

Nate Ledek had asked him to do a series of demonstrations at Mountain Mastery once he was settled in Montana. Ryan hadn't been particularly interested—until now. How would Joelle react? Would she enjoy the intensity of a shibari scene? Because the entire process was extremely intimate, and he'd want to make sure every inch of her sex was beautifully displayed for all to see. Hell, he was getting hard again despite having just experienced one of the most crushing orgasms of his life downstairs a few minutes earlier. He hadn't intended to fuck her after the flogging, but he'd had to open his leathers and take her or he'd have embarrassed himself in a way he hadn't since puberty. *Christ, if just thinking about how she'll look in ropes does this to me, I really need to get online and order some supplies.*

Stepping into the private room was like stepping back in time. The entire space was decorated in an old west motif reminiscent of every museum he'd been forced to visit as a kid. Ryan's mother took their Texas heritage seriously, he swore she'd dragged him from one end of the state to the other making sure he understood exactly how wonderful the Lone Star state was. Looking around the room, Ryan wondered if Miss Kitty had picked out the furnishings herself. "Christ, I feel like we've just walked onto a *Gunsmoke* set."

Brandt's laughter woke Joelle, and Ryan watched as her eyelids fluttered open as she took in her surroundings. "Wow, this is...well, it's just...we're still at the Prairie Winds Club, right? Because this sort of looks like a museum. And I'm not sure how I'd feel about being naked in a museum."

Ryan couldn't hold back his bark of laughter. "Hell, I was just thinking the same thing. Next time I'm choosing the room, we're not letting Marshall Dillon here decide."

"Har, har. You're a real comedian. Personally, I think you watch too much late night television, most people probably don't even take notice of this room." Ryan stared at his cousin in disbelief—he didn't think he knew anyone with an I.Q. over dull normal who wouldn't see the room and wonder what sort of movies had been shot inside. Ryan's teasing faded quickly when Brandt slid open a hidden panel and began flipping switches. A large screen lowered from the ceiling and flickered to life.

TOBI STOMPED HER foot in frustration. *Damn, they make me so stinking mad I could just spit.* Kent had scooped her up the minute she and Gracie stepped back into the main room after their conversation with Joelle. He'd begun herding her toward one of the more secluded areas of the club when she'd noticed someone setting up a stage. When she'd inquired about the scene, he'd told her it wasn't any of her concern and that's where things started to go south.

"I don't understand why you won't tell me who is doing the scene. Is it one of your old girlfriends or something?" The look he'd given her might have deterred a lesser woman, but sometimes Tobi didn't have the good sense to walk away from a fight.

"Be very careful, baby. You're getting dangerously close to the edge of my patience." *Oh yeah? Well, news flash for you, husband mine. I'm pretty close to my own limit. When you won't tell me what's going on it just makes me all the more curious.*

"Is that right, well, hell....o. Sure wouldn't want that, now would we?" He moved so quickly, all she saw was a black leather blur before he'd thrown over his shoulder. Well, it looked like he hadn't been kidding, his patience had indeed been hanging by a thread...a thread that seemed to have snapped. Even from her upside down position, she could tell he was heading out the back door. Damn and double damn, she'd hoped he'd, at least, stomp through the main room so she could get a glimpse of who was putting on the demonstration.

"Find my brother and tell him I need his help. I'll be waiting for him at the gazebo, but he better hurry it along." Kent's voice sounded rough and Tobi wasn't sure who he'd sent to find Kyle, but the young man's voice had been all breathless and sickeningly sweet with its "Yes, sir. Anything you say, sir." Good Lord, she wanted to gag. Hell, she was never going to be that kind of submissive. Cripes, so much for trying to go a whole week without a punishment paddling. The last she knew there was still some kind of betting pool among the club Masters about how long she'd make it each week. *They really should be donating all that extra money to charity if you ask me.*

The air blowing up the *pretend skirt* they'd given her to wear was warm, thank God Spring had decided to drop in on the Hill Country early this year. "You made it almost six days this week, kitten." Tobi shrieked in surprise as Kyle stepped out of the shadows as Kent moved down the path.

"Holy shit, you..." A stinging swat landed on her ass and she gasped as the heat spread quickly between her thighs.

"Watch your language, baby. I'm really not it the mood for you to push my boundaries." Kent was usually the easier going of the two of them, but something had clearly set him on edge and for some reason, Tobi didn't think it was her.

"I believe you were going to inquire how I knew where you were. Well, I was tipped off by the new fellow we have working in the control room. He is going to work out well I do believe." The smug tone laced through Kyle's voice told her he knew he was going to get to play *good cop* tonight and the jerk seemed to be looking forward to the change. *Fuck a fat fairy. There just isn't any way this is going to work out well for me.*

KENT WAS DAMNED glad Tobi couldn't see his face because he was having a hell of a time not laughing. One of her most endearing quirks was her habit of speaking her thoughts out loud when she was stressed. He and Kyle had worried she was breaking the habit because it hadn't happened in months, but evidently she was worried enough tonight the useful little *tell* had returned. Neither he nor Kyle cared if she knew her new friend was being flogged into subspace by Ryan Morgan, but they also knew the best way to set up the scene they had planned for their sub was to pique her curiosity a bit. Nothing got their willful wife in more trouble than her curiosity.

"Put me down you, big oaf. I'm getting motion sick hanging upside down. We all know you aren't going to do anything in that darned gazebo. It's too open and all those uptight ninnies on the river would have a conniption if they saw anything that might give them an erection. I swear some of those people need to get naked and nasty just to find out how much fun it is." Well hell, he couldn't put her down now because he couldn't wipe the damned grin off his face to save his soul.

Thank heaven his brother seemed to be maintaining some measure of decorum. "Well, kitten, I think you may find we've made some *improvements* to the gazebo. A few modifications that will allow us more opportunities to use it in a way we use the lovely facility we know you're so fond of." Oh yeah, they'd made changes alright. The electric privacy screen was a state of the art design allowing anyone inside the structure to see out but no one outside could see in. The retractable device was virtually hidden when not in place and could be set up remotely from an app on their phones.

Tobi's assessment was true of many of the boaters behind their property. It amazed him how *dedicated* the penis police were to anchoring behind the club on the weekends during fair weather. He knew they were hoping to catch a glimpse of the activities rumored to be taking place at Prairie Winds. He, Kyle, and their whole staff took every possible precaution to make sure they left each week disappointed.

Rounding the corner, Kent was pleased to see the gazebo had all but disappeared from view. If you didn't know where it was, you'd be hard pressed to find it; and that was exactly what he and Kyle had hoped to achieve. He set

Tobi on her feet and turned her slowly—her soft gasp told him she was surprised. "How? I can barely even see it and we're so close."

Moving forward quickly, Kyle opened the door and the three of them stepped into a sea of soft white fairy lights. The view of the riverfront from inside the gazebo was perfect. The light of the full moon illuminated the surface of the water making it shimmer with a vibrancy they'd have otherwise missed simply because they never wanted to give the gawkers a reason to snap their picture. They'd learned the hard way most of the clothing they chose for Tobi disappeared when photographed with a flash. Kent didn't even want to think about that particular fiasco.

Tobi started toward the perimeter but Kyle stopped her. If they let her start asking questions they'd spend most of their playtime explaining all about the fabric and mechanical features of the Prairie Winds Club's newest feature. Kent could practically hear the wheels of her quick mind spinning and knew there were probably a hundred questions bubbling their way to the surface—it was definitely time to get things started. "Come here, baby." She seemed startled out of her thoughts, but he was pleased she didn't hesitate to move back to him. Once she was standing in front of him, Kent didn't hesitate. *"Strip."*

MICAH DRAKE RECHECKED the information he'd received minutes ago before sending a quick text to everyone working on Joelle's case. They'd only had a few suspects left on the list Joelle had given them, and now they'd finally identified the person responsible for the break-in at her apartment and the attempted breach of her home in Pine

Creek. Micah agreed with the others, both attempts had been more about theft and intimidation than physical harm. But he also believed former Senator Helen Rodrick would step up the game she was playing now that all the major news agencies were chattering like magpies about Joelle Phillips' upcoming news conference. The former senator was the most corrupt politician in recent history, but her loyal followers continued to drink the Kool-Aid as if the news stories about the women were pure fiction.

Shaking his head, Micah sent a final message to all the club's security personnel. They didn't have any reason to believe Ms. Rodrick knew where Joelle was staying, but he sure as hell wasn't taking any chances. First thing in the morning the entire team was meeting to discuss the upcoming news conference. They'd enlisted some big players in both the news and medical communities as well as several celebrities who'd been touched by cancer in one way or another. The up side? Joelle's announcement was going to get the hype it deserved. The downside? The whole dog and pony show was going to be a fucking security nightmare.

Pushing back from the bank of computers he'd been monitoring, he put everything in the capable hands of the men waiting to take over and made his way downstairs. He was anxious to get his hands on his luscious wife. He and Jax had been looking forward to his week for a long time. He adored their daughter, but Deaga's mama deserved this well-earned adult time. He'd been watching Jax escort Gracie around the club for the past hour and it was easy to see she was becoming concerned by his absence. If things hadn't finally started falling into place he would have joined them much sooner, but even his impatient cock understood Joelle's safety was more important than another hour of playtime.

Walking up behind Gracie, Micah slid an arm around her pulling her against his chest. He loved the way she fit against him and her sweet gasp of surprise. "You should be careful, Sir. My Masters take exception to strange men having their hands on me. I'm not sure they'd appreciate the way your muscular arm is lifting my breasts to the point they may well pop out of this hooker Barbie dress they gave me to wear. I don't even want to think about the fact you've raised the hem of this little frock so high my pink bits are probably displayed for all to see." Micah chuckled against her ear, the saucy little sub was obviously wound up and ready to play.

"I think I'll take my chances, baby. I think you're worth the risk. Besides, I only see one Master and I think I can work with him to make sure you have an evening you'll never forget." He hoped like hell their calendar wasn't off, they'd all been devastated when Gracie miscarried a year ago, but they'd known her body needed time to heal so they'd been biding their time. But she'd recently gotten the green light from both of her doctors so they'd been tracking her fertility very closely. Dr. Brian Bennett and Dr. Kirk Evans were members of the club as well as excellent OB/GYNs and having physicians who understood the lifestyle saved a lot of embarrassing explanations.

Wrapping her in the shelter of his embrace, Micah moved so he could slide both hands under the fabric of her halter dress. The soft, sheer fabric did little to hide her peaked nipples and he wanted to moan in satisfaction as the hard nubbins traced a line of fire over his palms. "You are so fucking hot, baby. Your body was made for us, your heart had our names written on it before we ever met. He felt her shudder before a soft gasp of acquiescence whispered from between her soft rose-colored lips.

Micah looked at Jax, who was watching them, the fire in his eyes assuring Micah their plan was still firmly in place. Yes, indeed. They planned to love their sweet wife seven ways to Sunday and then after a nap they'd start again. She might view this week as a break from their adorable daughter, but to her husbands, it was "make a baby week." *They had a plan.*

GRACIE WANTED TO laugh out loud at the two Neanderthals she'd married. She knew they were itching to give Deaga a sibling. She wanted that too but losing the baby had shaken her confidence. What if she couldn't carry another child? What if something went wrong and she left her beautiful daughter without a mother? What if her husbands decided they wanted another child more than they wanted the woman who'd only given them one little girl? Pushing her worries aside, Gracie concentrated on staying in the moment. She'd promised Tobi she would try to reclaim the carefree spirit she'd been before the miscarriage. One of Tobi's best attributes was her ability to empathize without claiming to fully understand someone else's grief. She'd spent hours with Gracie doing nothing but holding her hand, and it had been exactly what Gracie needed most.

When she looked up at Jax, his eyes were filled with patient understanding. "Are you okay, cariño?" He'd always called her his beloved and even more importantly, he made her feel cherished.

Reaching up, she smoothed her hand down his face. He was so tall she was barely able to reach his tanned cheek and when he pulled her palm to his mouth pressing a kiss to its center she sighed. Both of her husbands worked tirelessly to make sure the people they cared about were safe, Gracie hoped Joelle appreciated everything the Prairie Winds team was doing for her. But all of that was something to think about later…right now all she cared about was pleasing the two men who'd sandwiched her between them. "I'm wonderful. And I'm blessed. But…" She saw him raise a brow at her question as his Dom face slid back into place. "Well, I'm horny."

Jax moved so quickly she'd barely blinked before he'd scooped her into his arms and was bounding up the curved spiral staircase. She could hear Micah's laughter from behind them and it washed away the doubts she'd let cloud her thoughts earlier. Gracie fully intended to follow Tobi's advice and live each moment as if she might not get another chance.

Chapter Eleven

Brandt studied Joelle as she watched her earlier scene being replayed on the large screen in their private room. The video switched between four different views at the touch of a button on the small remote he held in his hand. He zoomed in on her back as the leather strips slapped against her skin in a steady rhythm. The resolution was so clear you could see the lines left behind as the blood was drawn to the surface making her skin glow and color perfectly. When he switched to the front view, he zoomed in on her face making sure her eyes were centered on the large screen. "Look at you, minx. Your eyes tell me everything I need to know about how you were reacting to the scene."

"Ryan knew—he said your needed more, that you needed the bite of pain to *get there*. And there's the proof. Did you know this about yourself, minx?" Brandt bet she'd never been so deep in sub-space before tonight. She'd no doubt heard about it, and he knew she'd gotten a taste of it during her punishment scene at Mountain Mastery. But the look of wonder in her expression as she watched the tape told him Joelle had just discovered a whole new world.

"No. Well, I knew I needed *something* to find the magical headspace I heard the other subs talk about…but this? I wasn't even sure it really existed. I didn't know why my scenes never seemed to work before you and before

Ryan...but, this is pretty conclusive evidence." Aww, their little scientist was back in residence. They'd anticipated her need for proof, it was part of the reason they'd set this up. He and Ryan had laughed about the *fact* they'd actually met a woman who was as "fact driven" as they were—no small feat.

Brandt switched off the video and tossed the small remote to Ryan. Turning Joelle so she faced him, Brandt was surprised to see her eyes glassy with unshed tears. "Minx?" He heard the worry in his voice and hoped she had too. Even though he'd known her for a year, this level of emotion was so much more than the dance of attraction they'd been doing since they'd met. D/s relationships required so much more communication they were almost always stronger than those in the vanilla world. "Talk to us, Joelle. We can't help if we don't know what's upsetting you." Hell, he wanted nothing more than to wrap her in soft cotton and protect her from harm. If he'd been the one to put those tears in her eyes, he damned well wanted to know so he could avoid it in the future.

She reached one hand out to Ryan and placed the other directly over Brandt's heart. He felt the heat of her small hand like a brand on his skin. "They aren't sad tears...well, not really. They are tears of relief. I've always wondered what was wrong with me because I couldn't get to the place I'd heard the other subs talk about. I thought there was something wrong with me. But I kept catching glimpses of the people in the audience, and they were caught up in the scene. Do you understand what that means?" He knew it was a rhetorical question and he didn't make any attempt to answer, but he couldn't hold back the small smile he felt tip up the corners of his mouth. "Oh, of course, you do because Dom's don't have the same struggles to accept their kinks. But it's really difficult for women like me. We're taught from the cradle to be *good girls* to not rock the boat, to please those around us. Essentially we're trained to be submissive. But then we get into school and everything changes. We're encouraged to pursue a career and told we can have it all. And those concepts are so divergent it's confusing and basically a recipe for failure. Until you and Ryan showed me how to let go, I didn't think I'd ever be able to trust anyone enough to experience the ultimate joy of submission."

Brandt didn't say anything because there wasn't anything he needed to add—yet. There was a lot more they could show her—hell, there was a lot more they *would* show her. But right now she needed a chance to process everything happening in her life. She'd had already had a very intense scene tonight, and they weren't finished with her—not by a long shot.

When she finally pulled back, Brandt could see recognition in her eyes. And the icing on this sweet treat was her recognition both he and Ryan had given her the safety and security she'd needed to let go. They'd been preparing her for days to take them both, so he knew she was physically prepared. And now he could see she was emotionally ready as well. *It's time to claim her in the most intimate way possible.*

"I don't know about you, cousin, but I'm more than ready to play some more with our lovely sub." Brandt was grateful Ryan had redirected the moment. There would be plenty of time later for serious discussions about where the three of them saw this relationship heading. For now, he was looking forward to finally being able to slide balls deep into her sweet ass. She'd taken the largest of the plugs they'd gotten for her. Now he knew she was ready, he hoped like hell he'd be able to take things slow and easy rather than powering in to her out of sheer desperation.

Ryan moved her to the bed and Brandt wanted to smile when he heard his cousin command her to remove his clothes. Ry always did love having subs strip him, claiming the feel of their fingers smoothing over the surface of his skin enhanced his pleasure. Brandt couldn't hold back his smile, Ryan Morgan had always been brilliant, and he was also one of the most tactile guys he'd ever met. It actually made perfect sense he'dsense he'd become a physician—he certainly seemed to understand the power of touch. *I could probably learn a lot from him if my brain was actually getting enough blood flow to function.*

He pulled a small bottle of lube from the warmer and wrapped it in one of the hand towels on the ornate dark oak end table beside the bed. Dimming the lights just enough to set the mood, Brandt stepped up to the edge of the bed. Joelle was kneeling over Ryan's knees, leaning forward to take him between her kiss-swollen lips. "Jesus, Joseph, and sweet mother Mary, baby. Your mouth is lethal. Slow down or this is going to be over long before I want it to end." Brandt understood the desperate tone of Ryan's voice all too well. He'd been on the receiving end of Joelle's oral attention and knew exactly how quickly she could send a man over the edge.

Deciding he didn't want to miss the party, Brandt adjusted Joelle's position so she was completely open to his touch. He didn't think she'd even registered the move until he noticed the goose bumps move over the creamy flesh of her thighs. He trailed the backs of his fingers up and down the sensitive skin, grinning when the muscles underneath quivered. It was great to know she was so responsive to his touch. Dribbling the lube over her rear hole, Brandt massaged the slick fluid into the tight ring of muscles of her ass. In just a few seconds, he heard her groan and Brandt nearly burst out laughing when Ryan's eyes crossed.

"Fuck you, Brandt. You have no idea how close I just came to filling her sweet mouth with everything I have. Christ, get on with it already."

"Well, get her into position and let's play because she's far too tempting for me to resist any longer." Within seconds, Ryan had sheathed himself inside her sweet vagina and had her pulled tightly against his chest. "Minx, I want you to hold perfectly still. You can use your muscles to press back against me, but don't move your body until we give you permission." His voice already sounded strained and they were just beginning. How the hell was he going to get through this without coming completely apart at the seams?

Ryan rubbed his hand up and down her slender back, and Brandt could practically see her relaxing against his cousin's chest. Ry's eyes met his, letting Brandt know she was ready. Lubing himself before wiping his hands, Brandt pressed his tip against her and began the torturous process of pressing forward and retreating in small fractions until he worried the top of his head was going to blow off from the relentless heat and friction. He wasn't making progress as quickly as he'd hoped, and it finally occurred to him why.

Joelle had responded perfectly to verbal and tactile direction during scenes, but he and Ryan had both been concentrating so hard on maintaining their control they'd both been almost completely silent. "Minx, let me remind you that you have put yourself into our care, and that means your only job is to submit. Let us take you were you need to go."

Ryan obviously recognized where he'd been headed

because Brandt saw awareness dawn in his expression. "Your body is ours to pleasure, baby. Let your other Master in. You belong to us. You are ours to cherish, and a large part of that is giving you exactly what you need." Ryan cupped her face between his palms and the words had the desired effect.

"Take a deep breath and then press out as you let the air out nice and slow, minx." When she did exactly as he asked, the rigid ring of his corona slid past the tight ring of muscles and he felt her sweet groan all the way to his toes. *Christ, I've never fought so hard to maintain control in my entire life.* He fought an almost overwhelming desire to shove himself as deep as he could into her tight ass, the fire wrapping itself around his cock was so intense it bordered on painful. "So fucking tight. God damn, minx you are killing me."

"Oh, God. It hurts so good. But I don't think there is any more room at the inn." He'd have laughed at her sweet attempt at humor if he hadn't known she was only half kidding.

"No, baby. He's going to be very careful and then we'll set a pace that will steal your breath. You'll forget how hard you worked to get to that point and just fly with us." Brandt nodded over her should at Ryan and the two of them began slowly alternating between pulling back to allow the other to push forward making sure Joelle was always full. He had a dim awareness of Ryan's movement on the other side of the thin membrane separating them, but everything was quickly narrowing to a pinpoint and the only thing he could think of was Joelle's pleasure.

Brandt and Ryan had shared women often enough to anticipate each other's need and limits—and God knew it had never been more important than it was at this moment. Without ever breaking their rhythm, Ryan helped move Joelle up enough he'd be able to use his fingers to give her the last boost she'd need to fly over the edge with them. Brandt knew the exact moment Ryan's fingers made contact with Joelle's clit because her whole body tensed a split second before it locked down in a release so intense she pulled both men over with her.

So much for our reps as being Doms who were always consummate in their control—yeah, that just fucking flew out the window.

JOELLE WAS DROWNING in sensation. With Ryan's large cock already stretching her enough to make the walls of her vagina burn, she was sure it was going to be impossible for Brandt to push his way into her ass without ripping her in two. But the combination of Ryan's verbal seduction and Brandt's relentless preparation made it work. Their hands had been everywhere…soothing, teasing, and pushing her until she'd suddenly realized they were both as deep inside her as they could possibly get.

Her lips felt swollen from the bruising kisses Ryan had given her while Brandt had been moving deeper and deeper with each thrust. Joelle's mind was spinning wildly, but one thought kept coming back to the front of her mind. Would anything in her life ever be the same after tonight? She didn't think so.

Their ragged breathing, the smell of her arousal, and her own groans filled the air around them in a whirl of sexually charged energy unlike anything she'd ever known existed. She could feel her body spiraling into the stratosphere, and she was starting to worry she wouldn't survive the fall back to Earth. As if reading her mind, Ryan whispered against her ear, "Let go, baby. We'll catch you. We'll always catch you." He moved her away from his chest enough to slide his hand between them, and when his skillful fingers pinched her clit everything around her erupted in a symphony of color and light. Their shouts faded quickly to the background as Joelle hurtled through space watching brilliant light trace the paths of stars and flashes of light so bright it looked like the neon white lightening she'd seen illuminate every nook and cranny in the mountains last summer.

Feeling Brandt flood her ass with the hot jets of his release sent her over yet another peak and she hoped they'd be able to forgo condoms soon. She'd never had sex without one until tonight and now she felt a bit cheated she hadn't been able to feel Ryan's release in the same way. Collapsing against his chest, her breathing rasping in and out, Joelle fought to pull in enough oxygen to speak. "Wow. Just wow." *Very eloquent, Joelle. Boy, if that doesn't make them want to keep you around, I can't imagine what would.* She wondered how the demon on her shoulder expected her to be able to wax poetic when she was barely able to speak at all. Damn, sometimes the little voice was her worst critic.

Joelle had played in enough clubs to know Brandt's ministrations were a part of the aftercare she should have expected. But there was an added layer of attentiveness she didn't think was likely a part of his regular routine. *You're projecting, Joelle. Just because you want to believe you could be special to these men beyond this moment, won't make it true.* Her experience with men had been limited to a handful of boyfriends who'd set their sights on her trust fund and portfolio. They'd had little interest in her work, and as long as they could keep her locked in a lab somewhere things had been fine. But the minute she showed any kind of backbone or God forbid she appeared to be smarter than they were things went to hell in a big hurry.

Ryan used gentle hands to slide her off his chest and roll her toward Brandt. She'd been so lost in thought, she hadn't even realized he'd returned to the bed. Joelle heard the bathroom door snick closed and wanted to smile at how easily they worked together to make sure she wasn't alone after the intense scene they'd shared. Brandt's fingers traced a line down the side of her face and he pushed back the tendrils of hair that had escaped the clip.

"Amazing. Beautiful. Ours." She felt her eyes widen in surprise and he smiled. "I could practically hear all the insecurities and worries bouncing around in that brilliant mind of yours, minx. Some of those questions will only be answered with time. You'll eventually understand my cousin and I are both going to still be here when this mess blows over. There will definitely be logistics to work out because your work is too important to be pushed aside by living in Pine Creek. But that isn't going to be as big a challenge as you might think. What I do think might be a problem is making you believe our affection isn't something you have to *earn*."

Joelle felt the tears fill her eyes and she was helpless to hold them back. Rather than being put off by her display of emotion, Brandt gave her an understanding smile before pulling her into his arms. Over the past few years, Joelle had listened to other submissives discuss the emotional crash after intense scenes, but she'd never experienced it. She was quickly beginning to realize she had actually experienced very few of the benefits of the lifestyle she'd professed to follow. *It's like being a card-carrying member of a club, but you only attend a handful of meetings so you've never really known what was going on.* God in heaven, she hated the naggy voice in her head.

Surrounded by Brandt's warmth, Joelle was quickly slipping into sleep when she felt Ryan settle behind her. His warm breath whispered over the shell of her ear, his words barely registering in her sleep fogged mind. "Sleep for a while, baby. Tomorrow's going to be a big day." *Big day?*

Chapter Twelve

JOELLE STRETCHED OUT on the lounger letting the sun warm all her deliciously tender muscles. Tobi and Gracie were both nearby chattering about the request they'd gotten from the brother of someone named Taz to help set up specialty shops in his club, but Joelle hadn't really tuned in to their conversation. It was still cold in Montana and she'd looked forward to enjoying the warm sunshine while she had the chance. The sound of the waterfall splashing into the pool and the distant rumble of men's voices were the perfect background noise for some much needed down time.

"Hey, Joelle, how did you enjoy the Miss Kitty room?" Tobi's anxious voice cut through the haze clouding her Joelle's mind.

"Miss Kitty? Oh, the private room? Well, it was pretty authentic at first glance. Sort of like being naked in a museum, though, that was a little odd." Gracie burst out laughing causing Joelle to sit up quickly. "Damn. I'm sorry, Tobi, I hope I didn't hurt your feelings." Gracie's continued laughter didn't do anything to sooth Joelle's frayed nerves. *Shit!* The last thing she wanted to do was insult her new friend.

Tobi shook her head and grinned. "Nope didn't hurt my feelings a bit. I've been trying to get Marshall Dillon and Festus to get rid of that room for over a year. It's embarrassing, but for some reason, the Doms seem to like it. I'm really hoping Snoops-R-Us is tuned in to this channel and heard what you said because that's been my argument all along."

"Oh, I don't think there's much chance they aren't listening. There's someone new for us to corrupt, so they'll be zeroing in on each and every word…you can count on it." Gracie didn't seem terribly alarmed by their husband's obvious stalking, just very matter of fact.

"Does it ever bother you…being watched so closely, I mean?" Joelle didn't want to offend anyone, but the whole situation seemed almost like an episode of *Conspiracy Theory*.

Tobi rolled to her side and took a big gulp of her margarita before answering. "Honestly? Not as much as you might think. We know their hearts are in the right place and the truth is there are times their skepticism has saved our backsides. Neither Gracie or I had great childhoods, but we hadn't seen the worst of humanity either. The men, on the other hand, have a world of experience with the darker side of the human race."

Gracie sat up and smiled ruefully. "Even with the horrors I knew awaited me when I was being held by Raphael Baldamino near my home in Costa Rica, I was never exposed to the worst. The elderly doctor who helped my mother, brother and I escape paid for his good deed with his life." Joelle watched a single tear slide from beneath the Latin beauty's sunglasses and she instinctively reached out grasping Gracie's hand in her own giving her fingers a squeeze. "If they hadn't been listening, my pride would have kept them from having the information that ultimately saved us both." Her small hand elegantly waved in Tobi's direction and Joelle wondered how on Earth the two women had managed to find such trouble.

"What my sister-in-crime is trying to say is, too often we've gotten our ass…ets in a sling and being watched has pulled said ass…ets out of the fire. But I want it noted there are times having every word shared among the security staff is more than a little annoying." Tobi's honesty was so refreshing Joelle found herself smiling.

"Of course, I don't suppose either of you has used that extra mode of communication to your advantage, have you?" The blush that washed over Tobi's fair complexion was answer enough.

"Hello? Do we look dim-witted to you? Of course, we use any advantage we can, after all, we've each got two husbands. Two *alpha* males of the highest order husbands. Two sexually dominant husbands." Tobi waved her hand dismissively. "I could go on, but you get the idea. Drat, now we've probably given them all big heads." The sinister smile that traced over the pretty blonde's lips probably gave her husbands nightmares. "We may be submissive in our sex lives, but we're also building a successful business of our own."

Joelle smiled at her new friends and wished Coral was there, she had the feeling her newly married friend was going to really blossom now that she didn't have to spend so much time and energy looking over her shoulder. "Tell me about your business, I've picked up bits and pieces but I'd love to hear more about it from you."

"Oh Lord, now you've gone and done it." A woman's laughing voice sounded from behind her and Joelle turned quickly. She was startled to realize the elfin looking young woman had gotten so close without her being aware of her. "Woah, honey. I didn't mean to sneak up on you. I'm just such a shy and retiring little ole thing I forget how quiet I can be." The woman's eyes danced with mischief as Tobi and Gracie fell into the fakest coughing fits Joelle had ever witnessed…and the barely disguised profanity laced denials made both Joelle and the newcomer smile.

The tiny woman stuck out her hand introducing herself as Regi, the West's former Office Manager. "Happy as we are to see you Reg, what brings you out to Happy Acres?" Gracie and Tobi's affection for their friend was easy to see.

"My husbands let me tag along. They were called out here for a *consult*." Turning to Joelle, she grinned. "Evidently the powers that be think someone is under a huge amount of stress and may need medical attention." When Joelle groaned, all three women laughed.

"Holy fu…tile helmets. I'm so glad it's not me for once. Those docs Regi's married to can be relentless. And if they have six Doms pushing them? Oh sister, you are so gonna be naked and prodded in every way but the ones that make you smile."

"What? Hey, I don't need a doctor. And, I sure as hell don't need two. Damn, I am a doctor for heaven's sake. Why do I have to get naked for a couple of physicians I don't know? What about patient's rights? And who is talking about my medical condition? Haven't they heard about HIPPA? Good Lord, this just sucks big donkey dicks all the way around. I'm not stressed out. I'm just fine thank you very fucking much."

By this time all three women were laughing like hyenas and Joelle couldn't hold back her own chuckle. "Well, shit. Maybe I am strung a little tight, but I think calling in two doctors is really over the top. What I really need is a couple of really strong margaritas and maybe a massage. And not one of those that ends up being an insert body part A into slot C massage either. I mean a real massage by a trained therapist."

All three women stood up. "This we can arrange. Come on, you asked about our business. Well, this is a part of it. We've set up Forum Shops in clubs all around the country. And I happen to know our on-site massage therapist has kept her schedule open for us today." Tobi was leading the way and the rest of them fell in line behind her.

"As a matter of fact, we've signed a contract with Taz's brother, Nate. We'll be heading to Mountain Mastery in a few weeks to do a preliminary on-site. Taz has told him enough about what we've done here and he wants to do something similar in his own club. Have you heard of it?"

"Yes, indeed. And boy do I have a story to tell you." Joelle felt herself relax as they made their way to the club's on-site day spa. She was pleasantly surprised to see the spa was large enough to accommodate all four women at the same time. "I'm guessing your husbands are responsible for this facility being ready and waiting for us."

Gracie and Regi both grinned and said, "Kent" at the same time. Regi laughed. "Don't get me wrong, Kyle is a softy under all that *Lion King* persona. And, Kent's roar is just as dangerous as Kyle's, but it's also much more covert." Tobi skittered off to the back of the spa to the laser treatment area and Gracie went for a manicure leaving Regi and Joelle to settle onto side-by-side massage tables.

Regi's voice was more muffled now, but it was still easy enough to hear the tenderness in her voice when she spoke about her former bosses. "Kyle and Kent West gave me a job and looked after me even though they knew I wasn't who I pretended to be. How I thought I could fool a group of men, who'd made a career of unearthing the truth is still a mystery...even to me. I love them like brothers, Jax, and Micah, too. But it also means I know them, and this has Kent's name all over it. Kyle would simply order us to stay put, but Kent would make staying on-site so appealing we wouldn't want to leave."

Joelle moaned in anticipation as the massage therapist drizzled the warm sesame oil over her back. The scent of the oil was more pungent than she was accustomed to; but it was oddly medicinal and the tingling sensation spreading over her skin made Joelle wonder what the masseuse added to the mixture. "Makes perfect sense to me. I don't even feel particularly manipulated...maneuvered perhaps, but if the results were going to be the same, this is a much better way to go."

The therapist's hands were heavy and not particularly skillful. It surprised her that the Wests hadn't hired someone better. The fuzzy feeling inside her head made it impossible for her to think past the intense pressure being used to ease the knots in her back. *Hell, wait until you hit my ass and thighs...we may be here until dark before you work out all the kinks.* Chuckling mentally at her double innuendo, Joelle felt herself drifting into the sweet fuzzy place between being alert and comatose and barely registered the pin-prick against her oil-slicked skin.

JAX MCDONALD LISTENED as Kyle explained what the Templar and Prairie Winds teams had uncovered during the past twenty-four hours even though he'd been briefed earlier. It seemed their combined efforts had finally paid off. They had enough evidence to notify their local FBI office and everyone was now looking for the man Helen

Rodrick hired to retrieve the information from Joelle. Unfortunately for them, Joelle Freemont Phillips had turned out to be brilliant in more ways than one. She'd done a bang up job of hiding the documentation the man and his team had so far failed to find. Despite the fact they'd broken into her apartment and house, they were still empty handed. And he damned well intended for them to stay that way.

According to the former senator's latest communication, she had only asked the men to retrieve the formula. But Jax agreed with the rest of the team, the Presidential candidate definitely had more in mind than a simple theft. It was just a matter of time before she arranged something more personal to force Joelle's compliance—and their scheduled press conference was certainly going push the time table up exponentially.

Casually scanning the numerous security monitors lining the wall in the West brothers' office, Jax froze when he looked at the camera covering the back of the day spa. "Fuck! We've got a problem." Seeing the two massage therapists who'd worked at the small facility since it opened bound and gagged behind the building sent a fission of white-hot fear surging through him. In that split second, he was damned glad he was still sitting down because he wasn't sure his knees wouldn't have folded out from under him. Knowing his wife was in danger could level him faster than anything else in the world. Kyle was beside him in an instant tapping out commands on the adjacent keyboard and Micah had taken off out the door—no doubt heading to the club's main control center. Jax activated the wireless communication device he wore, his order to lock down the perimeter going out to every employee on duty.

Jax waited for what seemed like an eternity but was probably only a few seconds, until Micah announced he'd taken his place in the control room. Without missing a beat, Jax sprinted out of the West's office hitting the outside door with enough force to send it smashing into the wall behind it. He'd only covered half the distance to the spa when a woman's scream rent the air. Jesus, Joseph, and Mary his knees might still fold right out from under him. All the women in the small facility were important to him, but one of them was the center of his universe.

Before he rounded the corner of the hedge to get a visual on the spa he heard Tobi West shouting. "You bet your ass I'll shoot you. Set her down gently, right fucking now." Evidently whoever the little spitfire was talking to hadn't complied because the next thing he heard was the distinctive pop of her Sig Sauer P238. The small black pearl handled gun had been a gift from Lilly West—a gift Tobi's husbands had been none too pleased with. But they'd patiently taught Tobi everything she needed to know about the small, but extremely accurate weapon. And Jax knew she would have only used it as a last resort, but he was still completely stunned by what he saw as he rounded the last corner.

WITH TOBI'S LASER session completed, she joined Gracie for a manicure. During an unusual lull in their conversation, they'd looked at one another in question when they heard a muffled cry from the next room followed by what sounded like someone falling into the wall separating them from the massage therapy room. Tobi called out to her friends in an attempt to make sure they were both okay.

When they didn't answer, she was out of the manicurist's chair before the poor woman had even blinked. Rummaging to the bottom of her ginormous purse, Tobi pulled out the small semi-automatic pistol her mother-in-law had given her and flipped off the safety.

Tobi stepped into the hallway just in time to see a short, stout man with a swarthy complexion carrying Joelle toward the back door. She heard Gracie's frantic voice behind her and knew her friend was already sounding the alarm. It was obvious Joelle had been drugged, her body was far too lax for sleep. Tobi had learned the hard way how completely limp limbs became when drugs were involved, and right now Joelle looked more like a rag doll than a woman sleeping in a man's arms.

"Hey, ass wipe. Set her down gently and I won't shoot you." Okay, that might not have been the most polite approach, but she wasn't feeling particularly charitable.

"Fuck off, cunt. You won't shoot me—you probably can't hit the broad side of a barn and you'd be afraid of hurting your friend." There wasn't another word in the English language Tobi hated more than the one he'd just used. She narrowed her eyes as she heard Gracie suck in a breath behind her.

"You want to rephrase that, you dickless piece of monkey shit?" She noticed the taller man in front of Mr. Soon-to-be-mortally-wounded hunched shoulders shaking and he wanted to shoot him for just for laughing at her. "I'm not fucking kidding. Put her down. I will take you out and even if I don't you'll never make it off the property with her." Tobi had never been more grateful for all the damned security feeds in her whole life. And she knew what he didn't...she was a damned good shot. She would definitely hit what she was aiming at. Even though she wanted to shoot the man in the back of the head, she remembered Kyle complaining to his mother about not leaving suspects alive so they could be questioned. Sighing to herself, she reluctantly lowered the barrel of her Sig to the man's left knee.

They'd cleared the door so Tobi shouted hoping someone nearby would hear her. "Listen, this is your last warning. Set her down or I'm shooting, you ugly bastard. God damn it look what you've done. I'm cursing. I'm going to be in trouble and it's all your fault. Fucking put her down."

"Fuck off, bitch." *Bitch? Oh you just had to add that nasty assed frosting to already calling me the c-word, didn't you?* The sharp crack of her gun had sounded a fraction of a second before the man crumbled to the ground sending Joelle rolling across the soft grass. The first man turned to her with his gun raised, but he was too slow, and she shot the revolver out of his hand with a second shot into his shoulder…*just in case he decides to try again.*

The second man dropped to the ground screaming, as the world around her erupted into chaos. Shouts to lay down her gun sounded to her right, but she simply jerked her weapon in that direction until she saw Kent running toward her with his own gun in hand. She turned away from him, stalking toward the men writhing on the ground, fully focused on Joelle when Kent's arms came around her like bands of steel lifting her off her feet. Tobi had been so focused on getting to her new friend her mind didn't register who'd actually picked her up. Fighting for all she was worth, she squirmed in his arms, but he simply tightened his hold. "Let me go. I have to check on her. I think they drugged her. God damn it let me go."

"Stop." The sharp crack of Kent's voice sounded

against her ear, and Tobi instinctively responded. Relaxing in his arms, she felt herself sag. "Good girl. Sweetness, you scared another fucking decade off my life." He swept her up into his arms and turned to block her view of the screaming men she'd just shot. If their curses were to be believed, she'd probably need an exorcism or spirit cleanse or some other New Age treatment sometime soon. *I don't know what they're bitching about...it's not like I killed them. Geez, I didn't even shoot off any of the parts guys seem to think they can't live without.* Tobi managed to suppress the shudder she felt trying to work its way to the surface as the reality of what she'd done started to sink in.

Kyle seemed to appear out of nowhere reminding Tobi her husbands' skills as former Navy SEALs were never far below the surface. "Kitten, are you alright?" His fingers trailed down the side of her face with such care she couldn't help pressing closer into his touch. "I swear I don't know why we ever let you out of our sight." Tobi heard the mix of emotions in his voice and was grateful when Kent released her into Kyle's arms.

"I'm sorry I cursed. I was so scared he was going to take her." She heard her voice crack under the strain. She was afraid she was losing the battle to keep herself together. For several seconds she tried to shut out everything around her, absorbing as much of their strength as she could before facing all the questions she knew were coming. The sound of approaching sirens brought her out of the peaceful shelter of their arms. "Is Regi okay? She was in the same room with Joelle."

"Kirk and Brian have both checked on her. She seems to be coming around, but I'm worried about Joelle, she doesn't seem to be regaining consciousness as quickly." Tobi assumed they'd given Joelle a larger dose of whatever sedative they'd chosen, it would have been important to keep her as quiet as possible while they made their escape. She worried because most of those drugs were easily overdosed unless you really knew what you were doing. Kyle pushed the loose strands of her hair behind her ear and tilted her chin up so her eyes met his. "Kitten, in case I forget to tell you later when the shit hits the fan over this— I'm damned proud of you. And thank you for leaving them alive for us to interrogate, that's going to go a long way to help wrap this up." He pressed a kiss to her forehead and then turned her back into Kent's waiting arms. "I'm going to go run interference with local law enforcement until our FBI contact arrives. The feds aren't going to want these two falling under local jurisdiction."

Tobi didn't even pretend to understand, she just let Kent hold her knowing this situation was going to get a whole lot more complicated before it was all over. She was grateful their children were gone on vacation even though Kodi and Kameron hugs were pure healing magic. The next few hours were going to be challenging and right now she could use the distraction. Tobi knew she'd done the right thing, at the end of the day, she didn't like hurting other people, and having to rehash every second of it wasn't something she was looking forward to. She held on to Kent hoping he'd be able to infuse her with some of this strength as the sounds of sirens died suddenly replaced with slamming doors. A cavalry of outsiders was invading the grounds of the Prairie Winds Club and Tobi felt the adrenalin crash move over her like a tidal wave.

Chapter Thirteen

RYAN MORGAN WAS never more grateful for his friends and their connections than he'd been when they'd wheeled Joelle through the doors of the Lakeway Medical Center's emergency services. It was more than a little obvious how well respected the West's were when he was given access to information and services usually reserved for staff doctors or those with hospital privileges. Joelle missed the action since the asshole who'd been trying to kidnap her had pumped her full of some kind of sedative. Thank God he'd dropped her in the soft grass when Tobi blew his knee apart, the lush landscaping had prevented serious injury and she hadn't suffered anything more than a few scrapes. The residual effect of the drug she'd been given faded quickly once they started flushing her system with fluids. And now? Now she was being uncooperative to the point he was a hot minute away from giving her the paddling of a lifetime right there in the exam room.

"I'm fine. I want to leave. I hate hospitals. Well, I hate them if I can't leave. There isn't any reason I can't leave. You're a doctor, you can take care of me back at the Prairie Winds or we could go on to your place in Houston. I just don't see any reason for me to stay." Oh yeah, he was going to have to gag her first, *then* paddle her ass. God in heaven, she was worse than many of the soldiers he'd treated in the field.

Brandt had been leaning against the wall behind her in a deceptively nonchalant pose, but he finally pushed away, stepping into her line of sight. "Minx, I've known my cousin my entire life and I can tell you he is a hair's breath away from taking you in hand. Now, Dean and Dell West may be on the board of this place, and God knows they'd understand—but that doesn't mean everybody here is going to be thrilled about you getting your ass paddled in one of the emergency services exam rooms. And even though you have got that punishment coming in spades, I don't think these curtains are going to do much to cover up the sound of his palm warming up that beautiful, bare backside of yours."

Ryan heard her soft gasp of surprise and wanted to grin when her face flushed a lovely shade of scarlet. "I am not any more difficult than he is being stubborn. What good is it to have a boyfriend who is a doctor if I can't be released into his care?" The militant tilt to her chin was exactly the sort of gesture Doms associated with brats—*this needs to be nipped in the bud right now.*

Brandt must have sensed his ire because he flashed a quick hand signal to wait before grasping her chin with firm fingers. "Tell us what the real reason is you want so desperately to leave here? And even though I know you are well aware of the rules in a D/s relationship, I'm going to remind you anyway—lying by omission is no different than any other. We won't tolerate you lying to us or to yourself, so think carefully before you answer."

They both watched as she waged some kind of internal debate, worrying her lower lip while she seemed to weigh her words. When she finally started to speak, Ryan saw her eyes fill with unshed tears. "When my mom was sick, Dad and I spent a lot of time at the hospital. I wasn't old enough to fully understand how serious her condition was. But, I've never forgotten the haunted looks in the eyes of the patients or the fact she didn't come home. I can visit friends who are ill, but being a patient terrifies me." By the time she'd finished speaking, tears were racing down both of her cheeks and Ryan worried this was going to be the straw that broke her. The last thing he'd wanted to do was send her headfirst into an unpleasant memory. *Fuck me.*

Moving closer, Ryan took her hand in his hoping the physical connection would calm the trembling he'd seen in her hands. "Baby, why didn't you tell me this in the beginning? You could have saved us both a lot of aggravation. I understand why you want to leave, but we're still waiting for lab results for you and Regi. Until those come back, it would be irresponsible of me to ask them to discharge you." He hated seeing the disappointment in her eyes and hoped his alternative would help. "What I can do is give them both Brandt's and my cell phone contact information, then we'll take a walk around the facility so you won't feel so trapped. Tobi told me there is a lovely outdoor area between the buildings, let's get some fresh air."

The E.R. staff was more than happy to have their waiting room cleared out. By the time everyone waiting for Regi and Joelle gathered in the outdoor garden, there were over twenty people milling about the open area. Ryan was leaning against a rock wall lost in thought when Tobi West stepped up beside him. "Ryan, I have an idea."

Kyle stepped beside his petite wife and the look of horror on his face made Ryan smile. Kent and Kyle West's cool-under-pressure leadership style had become almost legendary among SEALs, so seeing Kyle blanch at his wife's comment made Ryan wonder how outlandish her idea could be.

Tobi's quick glance up at her husband had her rolling her eyes in a move Ryan was certain got her into trouble more often than not. As the owners of one of the country's most respected kink clubs, neither of them would be prone to ignoring gestures of blatant disrespect—particularly from their wife. "I know that look, Ryan. I'm not disrespecting Kyle, but we aren't in a scene or at the club, so he is *just my husband* right now. And besides…this really is a good idea. Dang it, I don't appreciate him going all pasty white every time I have an idea…it's just plain insulting."

Turning back to Ryan, she smiled. "Joelle looks like she could use a distraction and since her press conference is in two days, let's have her practice here. She'll get a chance to think about how she wants to answer the questions we all know she's going to face, and everyone here already knows what's coming anyway." Ryan was speechless for several seconds as his mind scrambled to find a reason to reject the suggestion, but it was a great idea for several reasons.

Kyle leaned down and kissed his wife soundly. "You are brilliant, kitten. It's a splendid idea, I'll get started rounding everyone up while Ry talks to Joelle." Turning to Ryan, he added, "If we're lucky someone will video this with their phone and post it. If it goes viral fast enough, she'll be much safer from those wanting to suppress her discovery."

Ryan chuckled. "Of course, every media outlet in the world will be knocking on her door—which translates to *your* door."

"You should probably add patients and their families from…well, from everywhere to the list of people who'll be clamoring for her here. But at least, no one will be trying to kidnap her and steal the information. Honestly, I really think she'll be able to relax once she turns it over to other researchers who will use it help people. She doesn't seem like the type to want the attention unless it's a means to an end." He hoped like hell Tobi was right because he and Brandt were already consulting with contractors and suppliers hoping to surprise her with a state of the art research lab in Pine Creek. Hell, if he and Brandt had their way they'd marry her today, but neither of them wanted to face their mothers if they eloped.

JOELLE WASN'T SURE how Tobi managed to do it, but she'd talked her into doing a "dress rehearsal" for the press conference, found her a change of clothes…all in the time it had taken Joelle to tame her hair and touch up her makeup. But damn if the little dynamo didn't give new meaning to the phrase *being steamrolled*. Within seconds of stepping in front of the small group of people who'd been rounded up for this impromptu question and answer practice session, Joelle found herself completely immersed in telling the story. It was cathartic to share the joy she'd been forced to hide for an entire year.

The questions she fielded were thoughtful and she could feel the excitement building in the room. She'd noticed several people taking videos and assumed it was to help give her feedback later. Joelle appreciated their effort, she'd often practiced her presentations to the Phillips Board of Directors using video feedback when she'd first taken over her own department in the research facility. As excited as she was to share the information, it was the looks of hope on the faces of the patients who had drifted into the garden to listen that made the past year's fear fade to insignificance. The looks of pride on Brandt's and Ryan's faces filled her with joy...looks like those were what decades of love were built on, but Joelle wasn't naïve enough to believe they'd want her forever.

The realization of how much her life had changed in the past year hit Joelle like a tsunami. Staring in Brandt and Ryan's direction, she felt the enormity of what she'd just done wash over her. Those videos weren't for feedback...they'd be on the internet within minutes if they weren't already live streamed. She'd just announced her findings to the entire world. Her knees started to buckle out from under her but strong arms wrapped around her. With her nose pressed into his chest, Joelle recognized Brandt by the outdoorsy scent of his soap. She had no idea how he'd reached her so quickly, but she was grateful he hadn't let her crumple to the ground like a fallen leaf.

"I've got you, minx. I've got you." She appreciated the fact he quickly stepped them both aside and she heard Ryan speaking to the group, but his words faded into the background. "Let's get you out of here before the hounds of hell descend. Hell, that's coming soon enough anyway." Grateful he hadn't carried her out of the room, Joelle lowered herself into a chair but didn't let go of his hand.

Before she could ask him any questions, Tobi and Gracie surrounded her. "Holy hand grenades, sister! You're going to blow up the internet...damn, Lilly is going to be jealous...she only blew up a boat."

"Yes, but the boat had two men in it, so you have to give her points for that since they were bad guys."

"There is that." Tobi's mock consideration was too much and Joelle felt a giggle bubbling up from deep inside. Before she knew it all the stress she'd been feeling a few moments earlier turned to an unpleasant memory. Tobi bumped against her arm bringing her back to the moment. "You rocked that, girl. I hope you don't mind we left out some of the details about the *rehearsal*." When Joelle looked over at her, she could see the worry in Tobi's eyes. "We all just want you to be safe, and this seemed like the best way to do it. You'll still have your big press moment in Houston, I promise. But this takes the pressure off and now they can round up that hussy former senator." She leaned closer and whispered, "I'll be in hot water if I tell you what I really think about her, let's just say it has to do with lady parts and waffles."

She must had looked confused because Gracie giggled. "We'll save the explanation for a girls' night margarita party. That way Tobi can explain and blame her language lapse on the tequila. It's one of the perks she gets for being a cute little blonde bundle of trouble, her hubbies are suckers for her when she's tipsy. We'll leave the discussion about the social implications of that for another day."

"Good Lord, Gracie. You can really get a stick up your butt sometimes. Like your men don't fall all over themselves every time you bat those killer eyelashes at them. Besides, now that we've signed the contract with Nate, we'll be in Joelle's neck of the woods in a few months so we'll be able to spend time together after this hurricane blows over."

Joelle couldn't hold it in any longer, she burst out laughing pulling them both close. "I can't tell you how much I appreciate you both. You've saved my sanity...and reminded me how important friends can be."

"Hey! What am I, chopped liver?" The sound of Coral's voice made Joelle jump to her feet. With a startled shriek, she threw herself into her friend's open arms. "Damn, I leave town for a few weeks and look at all the mischief you get yourself into. Good thing Tobi and Gracie have been looking out for you."

Joelle heard Sage's low chuckle behind her. "Well, my love, it seems you were right—I'm glad we made this little detour. But, I'm warning you, we aren't going home until this honeymoon is officially over. We'll just have to find some way to amuse ourselves at the Prairie Winds Club for a few days."

Coral whispered in Joelle's ear, the amusement easy to hear in her voice, "I swear the man is on a mission to knock me up before we get back to Montana." Joelle laughed at Coral's lame attempt at indignation. Honestly, she couldn't think of anyone who would be a better mother than her sweet friend.

Pulling back, Joelle looked at the people surrounding her and realized how wonderful it felt to be surrounded by people who actually cared about her. "Can we get out of here? I know there's a media firestorm coming and I'd like to be able to spend some quality time with the people I care about before all hell breaks loose."

"Amen to that, let's get the hell....ooooh, hi honey...out of here." Tobi batted her eyes at Kyle as he rolled his at her antics.

"Come on, kitten. Let's go before you get in any deeper." As they made their way to the exit, two vans pulled into the medical center's parking lot. Joelle heard curses muttered all around her, and found her view immediately blocked as the men surrounded her.

One by one, Coral, Tobi, and Gracie were ushered into the protective circle as they waited for their cars to be brought up. "Well, that didn't take long. I'm not sure whether to be impressed at how well my plan worked or pissed I underestimated how quickly this would spiral out of control. Clearly my scheme to take over the world still needs some refinement. It's possible my skills might not be developed enough for that particular project...*yet*." Joelle heard Kent West groan and Kyle cursed softly under his breath as Tobi looked over at her and winked. Joelle tried to stifle her laughter as she sent up a silent prayer of thanks for the distraction. *God, if you're listening, I want to be just like Tobi when I grow up.*

Chapter Fourteen

HELEN RODRICK STARED at the television vacillating between blind rage and stunned disbelief. Every news outlet was carrying the same story...Joelle Phillips speaking to a small group about her discovery was dominating the airways. The video had obviously been taken with a cell phone and was being touted as "leaked" footage before a scheduled formal announcement in a few days. *A leaked video my ass. The bitch is trying to draw first blood but she's got a lot to learn. It's not who makes the first cut...it's who is still standing at the end of the battle.* Helen had done her homework and this had Tobi West's name written all over it. The woman was a former low-level journalist who obviously still had a taste for a scoop. How two former Navy SEALs let that chunky blonde lead them around by their noses was a mystery to her. Helen knew all about their little black ops organization and they wouldn't be getting any more of Uncle Sam's money after she took office, she'd see to that first thing.

Watching the video as it was replayed on every news outlet in the fucking free world was making her insane. Wasn't there some sex scandal to splash all over the news? Hadn't her opponent done anything newsworthy in the past twenty-four hours? Christ, the man was a well-known philanderer, where the hell were the people she was paying to gather the dirt on him? God only knew no one would be reporting on her wild sex life. She'd need actually to *have* a sex life for anyone to make that particular discovery.

After the cheating scandals, she'd weathered with her ex, Helen had decided a good vibrator was a safer bet. Hell, the small battery powered device was usually more effective, too. How her ex-husband had managed to convince women to sleep with him more than once was a mystery for the ages. His looks had faded years ago, and he'd been steadfast in his refusal to have any plastic surgery no matter how many times she'd suggested it. After their divorce, he'd publically criticized her for her trips under the knife until her attorneys pointed out how expensive his little chats with the media were going to be.

Helen had flown into Houston late last night planning to meet with local media outlets and lay the groundwork to discredit Joelle Phillips prior to her scheduled news conference. She much preferred playing offense to defense, and now she was definitely in reactive mode. When the woman first reported her findings to the board, Helen started slowly liquidating specific holdings. But her candidacy meant she was under the microscope on several different fronts and making any sudden or noticeable changes to her portfolio would definitely draw unwanted attention. The last thing she needed was an investigation of insider trading. She'd already survived several scandals that would have sunk a lesser woman, she damned well wasn't going down on that ship.

Walter Phillips had promised her a meeting with his elusive daughter prior to her press conference, but she doubted he'd made any attempt to arrange it. And now the coward wasn't even taking her calls. His administrative troll insisted he was busy, but she didn't doubt for a minute he was avoiding her...and several other board members who hadn't wanted Joelle's discovery made public.

The man had obviously forgotten his company was no longer a privately held corporation. Surprisingly, Helen hadn't had any trouble unloading the Phillips stock she'd put up for sale two days ago. Damn that had been a stroke of luck, no doubt the price had just dropped considerably. When the sales of their cancer treatment drugs fell off, Phillips Pharmaceuticals would fold quickly.

Something the newscaster said drew her wandering attention back to the television. If she'd thought she had been stunned before, what she heard now shook her to her very core. *The FBI has confirmed they are currently investigating former senator and Presidential candidate Helen Rodrick in connection with the burglary of Joelle Phillips' apartment last year and the attempted kidnapping of Ms. Phillips today in Texas. Our source tells us agents are planning to interview Ms. Rodrick as soon as possible.* Anything else the journalist said was lost when there was a sharp knock on the door of her suite.

BRANDT STOOD ALONGSIDE Jax McDonald watching the large screen television as Helen Rodrick was led from her hotel suite by federal agents. "They could have interviewed her inside her suite." Brandt tried to keep the amusement out of his voice but knew he'd failed miserably when he saw the corner of Jax's mouth twitch up slightly.

"Yep—they sure could have." Jax's deep chuckle was all the confirmation Brandt needed to know how much Jax was enjoying the woman's obvious outrage as she tried in vain to jerk 'her arm out of one agent's grip.

"And it's interesting that a camera crew just happened

to be on hand, too."

"That is interesting, isn't it? I swear sometimes reporters can smell a story. Of course, there are times they need a little help, too—but don't take that as a confession."

Brandt wanted to laugh out loud. Jax McDonald was huge, almost seven-foot-tall and still built like the football player he'd once been. But the grin on his face was pure mischief—he looked like an eight year old trapped in a very large body. "Is your daughter as ornery as you are?" Brandt knew their little girl was her parents' pride and joy. He'd also heard she was brilliant as well as adorable.

"You have no idea. Hell, it's going to be hard to find out too. She's much too smart to give away all her secrets." The man's entire expression softened when he talked about Deaga and Brandt felt something tighten in his chest. *Jealousy? Envy?* Damn, he wanted to see look when he looked in the mirror every morning. He was tired of waiting—it seemed like he'd been waiting forever. He'd known the first time he and Ryan shared a woman exactly what he wanted—and now it almost was within his grasp.

When he looked back over at Jax, the other man was smiling at him. "I recognize that look, man. Don't let her slip away—I know the next couple of months are going to be crazy for her, but don't let the connection between the three of you suffer for it. Rack up all the damned travel miles it takes to keep her—it'll be worth it."

Brandt respected Jax, but they'd never been particularly close as friends go, but at this moment, the man was speaking directly to his heart. His response barely squeezed past the lump in his throat. "Understood and agreed. I've spent the past year walking a tight rope between trying to heal myself and slowly getting closer to her." And wasn't that the fucking understatement of the year.

He'd known she was hiding something when she'd first shown up in Pine Creek. He hadn't known what her secret was, but it hadn't taken him long to know it didn't matter. The one thing he'd known for sure was there wasn't anything he wouldn't do to help her. It shocked him to realize how easy it would have been to walk away from his family and career for the woman he'd come to think of as his own. He might have been willing to walk away from everything he held dear, but he'd also known deep down he wouldn't have to. His family would have had his back no matter what he'd decided to do, and somehow he'd always known he wouldn't have to make the choice.

"Enough of the heavy stuff, man. You're fucking up my happy vibe. Let's enjoy the view." Brandt had to agree with Jax, watching Helen Rodrick being led from her luxury hotel by the agents was satisfying, indeed. But he wasn't convinced this was going to be the end of the story.

JOELLE LEANED AGAINST the back of the sofa in the living room of the enormous living quarters on the top floor of the club. Taking a huge gulp of the margarita Tobi made her, shuddering as the tequila burned its way down her throat despite the beverage's icy texture. Joelle watched the local news replay the film clip of Helen Rodrick being led from the hotel and wondered what evil the woman was planning because her expression had been nothing short of murderous.

Gracie sat nearby but Joelle noticed she'd declined a margarita opting for a large glass of orange juice instead. Smiling to herself, Joelle was fairly certain if the pretty Latino wasn't pregnant already, she was likely planning to be soon. She felt a tinge of envy but pushed it aside quickly. Now wasn't the time to start thinking about the things she couldn't have. She was safe...and a lot of people were going to a tremendous amount of trouble to make sure she stayed that way. Joelle knew she should be counting her blessings not bemoaning the things she felt were slipping through her fingers.

Coral was sitting beside her and Joelle laughed out loud at her friend's scathing running commentary on the scene playing out on the large screen in front of them. "Damn, she looks like something that escaped from the seventh level of hell. Bet her ass is so puckered she sounds like a tea kettle when she farts." Tobi had been about to set a large platter of snacks on the square coffee table in front of them, but she froze at Coral's comment and for a few seconds Joelle wondered if Coral's off the cuff remark had been over the top. But the grin that spread over Tobi's face a split second before she burst into hysterical laughter erased Joelle's concern.

"Holy shiplap, that's classic. Damn, I knew there was a reason I liked you."

"*Kitten.*"

The warning tone of Kyle West's voice from across the room had Tobi wincing before batting her eyes at him. "Sorry, Sir." He rolled his eyes at her, obviously unimpressed with her half-hearted apology.

Regi hip checked Tobi aside and stuffed a piece of cheese into her mouth. "Won wok, Tob."

"Good Lord, Reg, I can't understand you when you are inhaling food. What's up with the starvin' Marvin imitation anyway? Are you knocked up or just planning head?" The look on Regi's face was something between a kid caught with their hand in the cookie jar and shock, but it had evidently been clear enough to have Tobi and Gracie dancing in place while hugging the tiny woman between them.

Within seconds, Regi's husbands were standing nearby, worried looks on their faces. A woman Joelle hadn't met sagged into the open seat next to Joelle and laughed. "Boy for a couple of obstetricians they're pretty uptight. But I guess I can see it in Brian's case." She leaned close and whispered, "His sister and her baby died during childbirth...that's why he became a doctor." Joelle blinked in surprise at the small blonde who'd so openly shared what most people would consider personal information. The woman grinned and extended her hand. "Hi, I'm Jen McCall. I am married to those two hotties over there." She indicated two men leaning against the wall listening intently to whatever Jax McDonald was saying. As if both men had felt their tiny wife's focus on them, they turned in unison to look directly at her—their desire for her was so thick you could almost feel it in the air. "I'll introduce you to them later, we all three work for the West's."

Joelle must have looked surprised because Tobi, Regi, and Gracie all laughed. "Don't let her looks fool you, the woman is a whole wrecking crew disguised as a harmless garden sprite." Tobi laughed and gave Jen a fist bump. "We're just grateful she likes us...she's damned dangerous when she's pissy."

"I don't get pissy. I get even...there's a difference." Jen's mock indignation hadn't been directed at anyone in particular, but her playful tone set Joelle at ease. As if she'd suddenly remembered something important, Jen turned her attention back to Tobi. "I heard you shot two guys and didn't kill either of them. Everybody knows you're a crack shot, so what's up with that?"

"You know exactly what that's about." Tobi looked between Coral and Joelle before shrugging. "Kyle and Kent seem to have a thing about being able to question the bad guys. Personally, I think it's a lot of useless yakking, but what do I know."

Joelle was sure she'd fallen through a rabbit hole and gotten trapped in some kind of weird alternate universe. But, Coral didn't seem to be suffering from the same confusion because she giggled at the other women's exchange. At least, she had been giggling until a long arm came over her shoulder snatching the drink out of her hand. "Does this have alcohol in it?" Sage Morgan's voice silenced everyone in the room. Joelle had seen the man have similar effects on almost everyone she knew back in Pine Creek.

Suddenly all of the men seemed to take an interest in what their women were drinking and Joelle found her own glass snatched from her hands. "Hey, I wasn't finished with that." *Almost, but there was still a sip or two left.*

"You are indeed finished with this." He took a sip of her drink and grimaced. "Good God, who made this? I've had margaritas in Mexico with less tequila." Looking over her shoulder, Joelle saw Brandt standing shoulder to shoulder with his brother. Wow, look at that. Damn if they don't have similar thunderous expressions. Who knew? *Wow, maybe that drink was a little on the strong side. Wonder if anyone else knows the room is tilting to the left.*

"My margaritas are tasty. Just ask anyone." Joelle tried to not grin at Tobi's petulant tone. "Don't you all have planning to do? World domination and terrifying small children don't just happen without a plan you know." Tobi yelped when Kent's palm landed solidly on her backside.

"Sweetness, I suggest you rein it in—quickly. There

were plans being made, but they had to do with our lovely subs. We've got something very special in the works for you all tonight." Kent's voice had an eerie tone, something between sickeningly sweet and deadly calm that made Joelle squirm in her seat. She'd heard that same tone from people her entire life...people who were being nice to her because they had to for one reason or another. Those same people often took any and every opportunity to undermine her whenever her father wasn't looking.

Joelle had always felt being wealthy was a mixed blessing. It was often impossible to distinguish between those people who genuinely liked you from those who were merely tolerant because they were being paid to. But there was something vaguely familiar about his voice too...something frightening that she couldn't put her finger on.

Brandt's warm hand on her shoulder brought her back to the moment and she was grateful he'd sensed her unease. Joelle looked down at her hands and realized the sharp pinch she'd felt was because she was twisting her fingers together so tightly they'd turned a ghostly shade of white. Looking up again, Joelle saw Ryan standing beside Kent West. His eyes never left hers but his words were for the man standing beside him. "What the fuck did you say to our woman, Kent? Damn, I don't think I've ever seen anyone turn quite that shade of terrified."

"Christ, I wasn't even talking to her. I was giving Tobi hell, not Joelle. Damn, darlin' are you okay? You are awfully pale." She could hear the concern in Kent's voice but before she was able to squeak out any words to reassure him she was alright Joelle felt another hand settle on her other shoulder.

This time, the hand squeezed ever so gently as heat

seemed to seep into her blood, spreading quickly and leaving peace in its wake. She might have been alarmed by the strange sensation if it hadn't been so utterly calming. "She's fine now. It was the edge of a bad memory, but it's been eased now. Remember little one, you're safe here. Master Kent's voice may have reminded you of the man at the spa, but they are nothing alike." Joelle felt like a puppet whose strings had been cut as she sagged deep into the sofa's soft cushions. Who was the man behind her and how had he known when she hadn't even remembered herself?

"Joelle, meet one of my loving husbands, Dr. Kirk Evans." Regi's voice sounded from nearby and Joelle realized she was blinking at her new friend in confusion. "He's not only a skilled physician but also an intuitive healer—a gift he shares with Taz. Not everyone can receive their gifts, but I can tell by the look on your face you're feeling all that sweet, feel-good energy washing the tension right out of you. Feels amazing doesn't it?" *Oh hell, yeah...now that I know what it is.*

"Doesn't work on me." Tobi's words sounded sullen, like a kid who wasn't able to reach the pedals on a bike as all her playmates rode theirs down the street.

"That's because your mind spins entirely too fast when your mouth is open...and your mouth is almost always open, pet." When had Kyle West stepped up beside his wife?

"I'm going to take that as a compliment, even if it did feel a little bit tainted." Tobi grinned as chuckles sounded around the room.

Kyle shook his head, but his smile told Joelle he wasn't really annoyed with his outspoken wife. "Let's break this up and reconvene by the pool at twenty-two hundred. Don't forget to pick up your supplies by the door." *Supplies? I really need to find my way back through that rabbit hole.*

Chapter Fifteen

"That's enormous, it's not going to fit." Joelle heard the alarm in her voice, but she hadn't been able to control it. *Shrill much?*

Brandt raised his brow and tilted his head to the side studying her. He didn't even need to say the words out loud because she already knew he was comparing the plug in his hand to his cock. She could have saved him the trouble; the plug was smaller than his enormous penis...barely. But damn, that rigid piece of silicone wasn't going to feel anything like Brandt and Ryan's silk covered steel heat. Would it have been too much to ask to find Doms who weren't so *blessed* physically? Shaking off her wandering mind, Joelle refocused on the men standing in front of her.

"I don't know where you went, baby, but I'd sure like to have been there with you. Your whole body is flushed, your pulse kicked up several notches, and you're practically panting. Yes indeed, I think I'd have enjoyed that mental road trip—a lot." Ryan's eyes danced with humor and for a few seconds she considered telling him what she'd been thinking, but Brandt took a step forward bringing her back to her senses.

"This plug is going to bring you a lot of pleasure later, minx. It's going in that delectable ass of yours or are you going to use your safe word?" Brandt's no nonsense tone had her shifting her gaze from the plug in his hand to his face. Good God, poets wrote sonnets about faces and bodies like his, and Ryan's were every bit as heart stopping. Licking her lips, her eyes moved over their bare chests. Neither of them had put on a shirt after showering and their faded jeans hung low on their hips. With the top buttons open it was easy to see neither of them had bothered with underwear. Their happy trails pointing directly to what she could see outlined clearly beneath the soft denim. *Can't we just skip the plug and just play with the real thing?* His lips tipped up at the corners ever so slightly. "I really am having trouble figuring out what you're thinking, minx."

"Bet I could narrate, but it would be more fun to hear it from our lovely sub. Come on, sweetheart, tell us all about why this plug is different." She wasn't fooled by the coaxing tone of Ryan's voice. Joelle knew a command when she heard one, no matter how sweetly it had been worded. They might both be sexual Dominants, but there wasn't a doubt in her mind they were both first class charmers as well. God save her from charming, gorgeous men who tempted her to dream of forever. Joelle knew she was going to have to return to the Phillips Pharmaceutical lab and then there would be weeks of testimony before every committee the FDA could pull together. She couldn't expect them to wait that long…even if they said they wanted to, it would be too much to ask. They'd both served their country and by their own admissions were ready to settle down. Why would they want to put those plans on hold when they could have any woman they wanted?

Blinking back the tears burning at the back of her eyes, Joelle took a deep breath. She was going to enjoy each and every moment she had with them before she was pulled back into the firestorm she'd created. If her discovery didn't hold so much hope for such a deserving population, she might be tempted to walk away and let other researchers follow up her research. None of it had ever been about recognition. It had always been about preventing others from losing the people they loved far too early. She'd wanted to prevent other children from knowing the pain of losing a parent, a husband or wife from losing the other half of their soul, or friend from losing the one person who could always make them smile. In Joelle's view, the recognition was more of a detriment than a reward.

"Minx, you're a very intelligent woman—I'm sure you recognized Master Ryan's comment for the command it was. Tell us what you're thinking."

RYAN WAS ENTHRALLED with the complicated woman standing in front of him. Her delectable body and sharp mind battled each other on a level so deep the struggle was holding her back in every aspect of her life. Her career had stalled because she'd tried to be compliant when told to shelve a project she passionately believed in, and her personal life was stalled because she'd lost the only person who had ever loved her unconditionally. And he could almost feel her fear now—she was worried about losing them.

Most women in her social and economic bracket learned at a young age how to hide or at the very least camouflage their emotions. The social functions a woman in her position were required to attend ordinarily gave them a lot of practice masking their feelings. But Joelle hadn't fallen prey to that never-ending circuit of parties and teas. She'd spent that time studying and researching, buried in books and hidden in laboratories searching for answers to one of the most important medical questions in history.

Standing back watching her fight back the tears threatening to fall as she fought an internal battle was one of the hardest things Ryan had ever done. He wanted to pull her into his arms and promise everything in her life would be smooth sailing from this point forward—but that wasn't a promise anyone could make. She needed to know that he nor Brandt would ever make promises they couldn't keep. For now, he was going to have to be content with listening every word she said—and to those she left unsaid as well.

JOELLE STEPPED INTO the circle of women she now counted as friends just in time to hear Tobi's exasperated complaint. "Yessirree, every woman's idea of a perfect party accessory…a sparkly piece of remote controlled plastic shoved up her butt. I'll bet they are on every debutante's must have list for their coming of age party. Heck, I'll bet they are going to be featured in Vogue next month. And that lovely wicked locking ring thing clamped around my clit? I'm pretty sure I read about that on a website devoted to Middle Ages torture devices." Joelle choked on the drink of water she'd just taken and tried to hold back her laughter.

"I think we need to expand our business to include more devices designed to *enhance our Doms' experience*. I swear if I hear that expression used one more time while my Masters are clamping something to my pink parts I'm going to need a shovel and an alibi."

Tobi looked up and grinned. "Well, welcome back,

Gracie. Where the hel..ck have you been? That Stepford Wife that was hanging around here was about to bore me to distraction."

Jen leaned in and whispered, "Keep it up you two and we're all going to be in deep doodoo, and I for one want to get this show on the road. Having the hood pulled back on my clit is making me want to do the nasty with one of those wacky little statues you all have hidden everywhere. And doing it with a concrete cherub is just *wrong* on so many levels."

Joelle and Coral both burst out laughing as the other three women looked on in confusion. Regi walked up grinning, laughter in her voice, "Oh this has all the makings of a great night. You two laughing and the Three Stooges over there looking baffled, like they don't have a clue why. Nobody's falling for that b.s. by the way." She started to sit on the edge of a planter but winced and stood back up quickly. "Okay, the perfect evening scenario might have a few flaws."

Coral looked down at herself and groaned. "One of those bumps in the road might be the fact I look like a boiled egg wearing rubber bands. I might have gotten a good tan laying on the beach, but I gained so much weight I'm not going to be able to fit into any of my clothes back home."

Joelle looked over at her friend and it did seem as if she'd gained some much-needed weight. "You look wonderful, you really were too thin before. Now you look healthy and so happy I keep expecting you to break out singing *Happiest Girl in the Whole U.S.A.* any minute."

"Ha and Jen's going to sing *Kiss an Angel Good Morning*," Regi laughed.

Jen groaned. "I thinking this is a night for something a

little less subtle. I'm thinking *Sexual Eruption* or *Give it to Me*."

"I think my Masters should put us in charge of the play list, I'd go for *I Wanna Sex You Up* or *Red Light Special*. We really need to make a list of all the sexy songs we like." Tobi was practically bouncing with excitement and Joelle laughed at how contagious the woman's energy was.

"I like *Afternoon Delight*, damn the Starland Vocal Band's harmonies are heaven sent.

"It's *I Want Your Sex* by George Michael for me. That's a wet panty song if there ever was one." Joelle had always loved that particular song, its lyrics about the beauty of sex and monogamy brought a deeper level of emotion to what was already a seductive melody.

Just then the music coming from the poolside speakers changed and Bob Dylan's *Lay Lady Lay* drifted around them like a warm caress. Gracie laughed. "I'd say that's the guys in the control room letting us know we forgot one of their favorites."

Coral tugged on the PVC tape Sage had strategically wrapped around her new curves. "None of these pieces are very darned long. I don't have a good feeling about this, I gotta tell ya. I'm pretty sure my round self is going to be bouncing out in the open before long." Yeah, Joelle had the same feeling, but the good thing was they were all in the same pickle.

Looking over where the men stood laughing and talking amongst themselves, it was fascinating to watch as each one of them subtly tracked their sub's every move. The scientist in her couldn't resist testing her theory. She'd only managed to take three steps toward the door of the club before a strong hand gripped her elbow and Brandt's warm breath brushed the shell of her ear, "Where are you going, minx?"

Before she could answer, Kyle West's voice boomed over the music. "Your attention, please. I believe we're ready to start. In celebration of the upcoming Olympic Games, we've designed a few games of our own. Subs if you would please all move to the other side of the pool, Master Nate from Mountain Mastery will help you prepare for this evening's festivities. *Prepare? I'm not sure I'm going to be able to take any more preparation without melting into a puddle.*

"Go on, minx. Master Nate knows exactly how you are to be prepped." She must have looked worried because he pulled her back and pushed her hair behind her ear with gentle fingers.

"This evening is all about fun, baby. You'll have a great time if you just allow your mind to let go of everything you're convinced you are supposed to be thinking about. Just let go and roll with it." She tried to smile at Ryan but felt her teeth biting down on her lip as nerves threatened to send her running back to their bungalow.

"I'm terrible at games. I've always been a hazard to anyone close when physical activity was involved." She'd grown up in a home that was more of a museum than a place to live and academics had always taken precedence over play. She'd wanted to learn to dance, but her father had insisted swimming was the only athletic skill she needed since it might one day save her life. As a result, the only place her lack of coordination didn't endanger others was while suspended weightless in water.

Taking a big breath, Joelle tried to corral her rioting emotions. Looking at the men who had been so patient and supportive she felt a pang of guilt. She seemed to be doing a lot more taking than giving...and she needed to stop before they decided she was more trouble than she was worth sooner than necessary. Leaning forward, she kissed them each on the cheek. Their startled expressions let her know how little she'd been putting into the relationship and she vowed to change that from this point forward. Even though they would probably only be together a few more days, Joelle wanted both Ryan and Brandt to know how much their time together meant to her. "I promise to try, not because I think I'm going to suddenly turn into an Olympic athlete, but because you are worth it."

THEY'D BOTH HEARD the emotion in her voice and first one and then the other pulled her into a prolonged hug. "Love, we don't need your thanks. What we need is for you to open your heart. We aren't fair weather boyfriends who are going to walk away because things are challenging for a while. We want much, much more from you, but we'll have plenty of time to discuss that on the drive to Houston." He'd seen her eyes widen at his change in pet names for her, and he hoped the subtle change set the tone for what they had planned for her later.

As Joelle hurried off to join her friends, Brandt shifted trying to ease some of the pressure as his erection pressed painfully against the zipper of his leather pants. "Damn, everything about her makes me want to pound my chest like fucking Tarzan and scream '*Mine!*' at the top of my lungs. I've never had a reaction like this to a woman." Brandt didn't consider himself particularly prone to emotion, but Joelle brought out feelings in him he hadn't even realized he'd been missing. The need he felt to protect her was a given, but in all honesty, he felt that same urge with Coral, Charlotte, and his mother. But there was something different with Joelle, a deep seeded need to help her reach all of her goals—to ensure that when she reached her twilight years, she looked back on their time together and knew he'd supported her in every way he could.

"I'm right there with you. I knew there was something special about her the first time we met and I hated leaving the country before I could explore it further. But now I know it was probably divine providence—I might not have completed medical school and you wouldn't have had the time to develop a solid foundation with her."

Brandt could almost feel the power of Ryan's attraction to Joelle pulse around them, the air was practically electrified with their combined desire for the woman who was disappearing into the darkness of the hedges surrounding the pool. Ryan shook his head and grinned. For just a second, Ryan looked like the kid Brandt remembered—the boy raised in the city but who felt more at home on his uncle's ranch. The rich kid who hadn't fit in with the other kids at his private school but who'd made friends easily each summer in Montana. The teen who had earned his bachelor's degree before he was old enough to drive.

"Do you remember the night your dad called all six of us out on the back deck? He said he wanted to make sure we all understood a few things about women?"

Brant couldn't help but laugh. Damn straight his remembered. Sage had broken up with his girlfriend over the phone and Dad had taken his precious first born down several pegs during one of their dad's rare closed-door sessions in his office. "Yeah, I think we had Sage to thank for that particular discussion."

Ryan laughed. "God, I was so scared he'd found out about something we'd done. Hell, I don't even remember which particular moment of insanity I was worried about because we had some very real *oh shit* moments. But something he said that night stuck with me. I didn't understand it at the time—hell, I didn't even agree with him but for once I was smart enough to keep my mouth shut." They both laughed because Ryan's intelligence and out-spoken nature had gotten him into plenty of trouble as a kid. "He told us there was a thing called the 'male code.'"

Brandt remembered the conversation, but having watched his two older brothers stumble through their first years of dating, he'd been at an advantage. He'd already noticed the difference in the way his brothers dealt with the young women they dated and the way his dad interacted with their mom.

"I never forgot what he said about the different rules of engagement for good girls and bad girls. Hell, at that time I was only interested in the bad girls. I'd often wondered about the validity of his statement. Fuck me, I thought my friends had lost their damned minds when they fell all over themselves after meeting the women they later married. But now, with Joelle, it's so damned obvious he was right—shit, it's just real fucking humbling I have to tell you." Brandt smiled because the simple truth was, his dad was rarely wrong—about anything. They were both still staring at the hole in the hedge where Joelle had disappeared like a couple of lovesick fools.

Ryan turned to him and for the first time Brandt could remember, his cousin looked unsure of himself. "I hope like hell she accepts our collar—I want her tied to us as closely as possible before the world sweeps in and tries to steal her from us." *From your mouth to God's ears, cousin. From your mouth to God's ears.*

Chapter Sixteen

JOELLE WAS THE last one to join the group and as she stepped up, she heard Tobi gasp. Anything that surprised Tobi West had to be over the top and without even thinking Joelle took a step back. Without turning his head, Master Nate's one word command to stop froze her in place. "You of all people should know how I operate, Joelle. Tell the others what I routinely tell the submissives at Mountain Mastery when they are presented with a situation out of their comfort zone."

She'd heard the words dozens of times so they crossed her lips without her brain even taking the time to fully process his demand. "You always have at least two options. Submit or use your safe word. Safe and sane are always important, but if the emphasis is on consensual those two elements are a given."

His eyes softened and his nod of approval made her blush. "You honor me and your Masters, sweetie." Turning his attention back to the rest of the group, his smile turned much more sinister. "Now, your Doms have gone to quite a lot of trouble to plan this evening's fun and games—it seems to me you owe it to them to at least try."

The man standing beside Nate had been introduced to Joelle as his younger brother Taz. *Who names a baby Taz?* Joelle didn't even want to think about the teasing he'd endured because of his crazy moniker. There seemed to be several years difference between the Ledek brothers' ages and Joelle wondered briefly about their backgrounds. Taz was close to six and a half feet tall and totally ripped. His biceps were enormous and during her little mental road trip, Joelle wondered where on Earth he found shirts to fit muscular physique. He must have felt her stare because when her wandering eyes finally made their way up to his face, Taz was making a less than stellar attempt not to grin. *Wonderful. Now I'll be in trouble for drooling over Master Nate's kid brother.*

TAZ KNEW JOELLE Phillips was trying to figure out the age difference between him and his brother. But she was also making what he worried were accurate observations about the subtle differences between them. Her look wasn't lustful, it was honest appreciation and Taz was wise enough to take it as the compliment it was without reading anything else into it. He'd been amazed at how open her mind had been when he'd brushed against her—it had been like stepping into a library that never closes. Everything on that level was organized, filed, and cross-referenced. It had been the emotional side that looked like a Middle Eastern market place taken over by a band of wild monkeys. It was easy to see why Brandt and Ryan wanted to distract her tonight. The formal press conference was only going to add to the emotional chaos.

Listening as his brother explained some of the basic rules for tonight's activities, Taz found himself laughing at the expressions on the sub's faces. Jen McCall was shaking her head and laughing, no doubt wondering what kind of pandemonium would follow their plan to mix tasks and unrelenting sexual stimulation. He'd wondered many times how her men kept her safe. The team's secret—very secret—code name for her was Miley. She'd more than earned the small nod to the *Wrecking Ball* songstress.

Gracie, on the other hand, had just shrugged and told the others they should be grateful she wasn't any real competition. If Jax and Micah hadn't already alerted him to the fact they suspected she was pregnant, he might have taken exception to her comment. But Taz planned to keep very close tabs on the little Latina beauty. He'd been in the gym working out when she'd come in to walk around the indoor track a few weeks after her miscarriage. Taz had subconsciously been monitoring her progress and when she failed to round the corner bringing her back into his view when she should have, he'd gone to investigate. What he'd found had almost torn his heart in two. Gracie was huddled in a dimly lit corner at the back of the building her delicate body racked by deep gut wrenching sobs. Taz hadn't hesitated, sitting beside her on the floor he'd just gathered her close and held her.

He could have used his power as a healer to cut through her grief, but he'd known the tears were more about cleansing than grief. She hadn't needed anything except the barest minimum of human contact—something her husbands were too invested to provide. They loved their wife to the depth of their toes, but it was that intensity that kept her from being able to let all the pain she felt bubble to the surface. She'd been holding in her anguish in a misguided attempt to spare the people she loved. He'd encouraged her to tell Jax and Micah how much she was struggling, assuring her they'd be hurt if she found out she was suffering in silence. He'd also gone against everything he'd ever learned about being a Dom by promising to keep what had happened in confidence unless he became concerned for her safety.

Gracie had kept her promise and Taz had been relieved when both men thanked him for helping open a much-needed line of communication. The incident had been a significant lesson in the importance of simple compassion—a concept his Native American grandmother had emphasized during so many of her training sessions. Taz wasn't sure which of them had learned the most that afternoon, but one thing he did know—he and Gracie had forged a close friendship he cherished. He'd definitely be watching her very closely and he wouldn't hesitate to pull her out before an activity if he felt his brother was going too far—and knowing Nate as he did, it was more likely than not.

Nate had been asking him to move to Montana for a couple of years, but Taz had been focused on staying close to his grandmother. Her wisdom and guidance as a tribal healer had been instrumental in Taz's development as a healer, but now that she was gone he was seriously considering the move. He'd still be a member of the Wests' black ops teams, but he'd already planned to cut back on those assignments. His body liked to remind him he wasn't getting any younger, the years of mixed martial arts training hadn't been particularly easy.

"Computer generated random commands? Who dreams up this shit?" Tobi West's voice brought Taz back to the moment. She turned her attention from Nate to Gracie. "Can't you keep Micah busy enough that he doesn't have time to dream up new ways to torture us? Good Lord, have I taught you nothing? Act out for flippin' Pete's sake, if he was busy paddling your ass the rest of us wouldn't be in this predicament. Take one for the team for crying out loud."

Gracie just smiled. "Master Nate didn't say this was my Masters doing? There are other people around with computer skills you know." Taz wanted to laugh because she was right. Each device the men had used on their lovely subs was remote controlled by a master program the likes of which Taz could hardly comprehend. But it wasn't Micah Drake's invention—no the credit for this particular piece of brilliance went to Phoenix Morgan. For once it seemed one of the world's leading on-line game designers had focused his attention on a whole new kind of pleasure.

THEY STUCK SOMETHING *up my ass that is remotely controlled by a computer?* The harpy part of Joelle's brain stuck in the 1940's couldn't let go of how impersonal it seemed to have a computer managing her pleasure. She had to agree with Tobi, whoever dreamt this up really needed a damned hobby…well, a different hobby at least. Listening to Tobi was a good distraction but it was Master Nate's comment that had Joelle dropping her jaw shocked clear to her toes.

"Quiet you two before I introduce you to the cock swings before we've even started." Both women blinked at him in question as Joelle groaned. His laughter was positively sinister sounding and his smile actually reached his eyes as he arched his brow at her. "Joelle, why don't you enlighten your friends? I brought several with me as a gift for the Prairie Winds Club." How very generous of him…geez, Tobi was going to go completely postal when she got wind of Master Nate's deceptively simple punishment device.

Taking a deep breath, she turned to the other women

and tried to avoid Coral's questioning look. "It's a narrow piece of wood suspended from the ceiling with a dildo...usually, a really large dildo mounted in the center or back. Master Nate or a Dungeon Master have the only remote control." She paused for a minute to take a deep breath. Joelle had only been sent to the swings at Mountain Mastery once, but she sure hadn't forgotten the conflicting emotions she felt. "The swing is raised until you are dancing on the tips of your toes and then the diabolical torture begins. It's equal parts arousing and embarrassing." She probably hadn't needed to add that last part, and if Master Nate's expression was anything to go by, he'd enjoyed her admission a little too much. Damn it, she'd just told him how effective the devious devices were.

Once Nate Ledek's attention turned back to the group, Coral bumped her shoulder against Joelle's. "You and I are going to have a very long chat, my friend. Yes...a *very* long chat." *Not looking forward to that...nope, not even a little.* Coral was a sweet girl with the heart of a warrior and Joelle knew she wasn't going to like being left out of such an interesting loop. Probably going to be pretty difficult to explain to the only friend she'd had for the past year that her weekend trips out of town had been spent at a kink club. It didn't seem like the sort of thing Coral was going to view as an oversight.

"Micah doesn't get credit for this gift, you can thank Coral's brother-in-law for this fun gadget."

Coral's gasp was followed quickly by a curse. "You just wait until I see that rat. A computer controlled butt plug? What the holy heck was he thinking? And the little piece of plastic wrapped around my clit? Knowing it's responding to a bunch of code written by my brother-in-law makes me wonder what his dates are like." Coral's entire body shuddered as everyone around them burst out laughing.

Hell, even Master Nate hadn't been able to hold back his chuckle. "Now, let's get you moved back to the pool area. The first game is all about balance and poise under pressure. Are you ready?" *He can't be serious.* There wasn't a chance in hell Joelle was ready for this, but at least, none of the others appeared to be enthused either. "And don't forget, any Dom who sees inappropriate behavior can send you to the swings or take a piece of your lovely PVC tape as a *fine* for the offense." Oh yeah, like there was any chance they'd forget their Doms had conveniently built in ways of ensuring they were all going to be naked as jay birds in ten minutes or less.

Joelle had been wrong, she'd managed to keep her skimpy pieces of PVC tape for twelve minutes and forty-five seconds...not that she'd been counting. It hadn't surprised anyone that Tobi West was the first one naked and Jen hadn't lasted much longer. Everyone laughed when Sam McCall handed his brother a hundred-dollar bill. Sage shook his head laughing. "I told you she wouldn't last more than a hot minute."

Tobi and Jen had both fallen in the pool in a display Joelle was sure would be shown in BDSM circles for years to come because there wasn't a chance in hell the Doms were going to erase *that* video. Pleasure had blindsided Tobi when her plug started what she'd described as a "tap dance with dynamite" and she'd fallen ass over teakettle into the water. Somehow she'd managed to launch the tray of drinks she'd been carrying the entire length of the narrow bridge the club's dungeon monitors had built over the water. She'd surfaced cursing like a sailor before the ice from the beverages stopped tumbling across the pool deck.

Jen lost her balance and fell over the pool's edge because she'd been laughing so hard at Tobi. Joelle and Coral had both watched in stunned silence and Gracie quietly narrated the comedy playing out in front of them. "Nobody is going to convince me that program is entirely random. Even Tobi isn't that much of a trouble magnet. And anyone with an ounce of common sense knew she'd end up in the pool. I love her like a sister, but she can get herself into a mess quicker than anybody else I know. And Jen? Well, that part was just plain funny." The entire scene reminded Joelle of a Carol Burnett skit. *Damn, that was one of the funniest things I've ever seen.*

Regi leaned over to Joelle and whispered, "I'm so glad that wasn't me. I really don't swim very well…okay, that's not really true. I can't swim at all. Even my Masters don't know that…"

Joelle turned to her quickly. "I won't let you drown, I promise." The relief was easy to see in Regi's face. "But, sweetie, you really need to tell your husbands about this, because I'm pretty sure they'll consider it a big deal." *Massive understatements aren't sins, are they? Because if they are, I'm probably going to a whole new level of hell now.* Joelle had played enough to know Doms in committed relationships with submissives demanded to know every detail when their sub's safety was at stake. And a play party beside a pool when a sub wasn't able to swim would definitely be considered a huge issue.

Coral let out a yelp of surprise beside them and the tray of drinks she'd been holding tilted precariously to the side. Without thinking, Joelle reached over to steady her friend earning her a sharp reprimand from Master Nate. She'd been standing out of Ryan and Brandt's view, but her faux pas hadn't escaped the man running the show. "You aren't allowed to help. I believe that directive was quite clear.

The only reason I'm modifying the punishment is I'm convinced your action was reflex rather than deliberate insubordination." *Insubordination? Geez, once a soldier, always a soldier.* "Turn around."

Master Nate gave her two harsh swats, one to each cheek of her ass and then cut the PVC tape in an arch up from one hip then down to the other, displaying what she was sure were two crimson handprints on her backside. The rat bastard didn't have to tell Ryan or Brandt she'd gotten into trouble—they'd be able to see it clearly for themselves. *Jerk. Should have known better than to think he'd be charitable.*

Chapter Seventeen

Phoenix watched the monitors from the main control room of the Prairie Winds Club as the first two submissives fell into the pool. Nate hadn't lied to the women when he said the program was run by a random computer algorithm, but he'd also neglected to mention it allowed for impromptu intervention as well. "Shit, I didn't see that coming." He recognized the curvy blonde who'd plunged headfirst into the water as Tobi West, but he wasn't sure about the second woman's identity until the man next to him called her Jen.

Mitch Ames had volunteered to help monitor the evening's activities when he'd heard Phoenix was going to be on-site. They'd met a few years ago at a gaming convention. Phoenix had been surprised to learn his friend had been a Green Beret—it had been completely erased from his online biography. Evidently Mitch and the U.S. government were in agreement on at least one point—burying their connection was in both their best interests.

"Don't worry about Jen, she's working on special assignments with the black ops teams. She's so close to reckless it's terrifying, but she's smart as a whip and everybody underestimates her. Honestly, falling in like that is pretty typical. Sam swears most of her kills while on assignments have been accidental. Personally, I think her real superpower is making the shit she does *look accidental.*"

Phoenix laughed as he zeroed in on the exchange between Nate and Joelle. "Damn, buddy, putting your hands on my future sister-in-law is a good way to get your ass kicked. My brother and cousin only share with each other."

"You think Brandt and Ry are going to get this one wrapped up? She's got the potential to have a huge impact on the medical world."

He understood Mitch's concern, but Phoenix knew the two men who'd claimed her had no intention of standing between Joelle and her destiny. But they weren't going to let her go either. "They're already working on a state of the art lab for her in Pine Creek. I think you'll see the Montana and Texas Morgans pool their resources very soon. The newly formed Morgan Holdings is poised to have a vested interest in medical research." Yeah, times were definitely changing and Phoenix was enjoying his front row seat without feeling any need to be the one in the spotlight.

"Any progress finding Athena?" Mitch knew the woman who'd bested them both in online games was a thorn in Phoenix's side. Damn it, any women with the audacity to name her online persona after the Greek goddess of wisdom and war strategy should have enough common sense to know she'd be seen as a challenge once she'd bested the game's designer.

"No. But I haven't had much time to look either. My brothers' love lives keep interfering with my own social calendar. Damn, I hope the next one falls for some boring librarian who's never been out of the state and doesn't have an enemy one."

"Dreamer." The amusement in Mitch's voice made Phoenix smile. The two of them had discovered early on they had very similar interests and tastes in women. They also both came from wealthy families. But Phoenix had amassed a fortune of his own so he had plenty to play with, Mitch viewed money as a convenience to be used and not stored away in a bank vault waiting for a mythical coming disaster. Phoenix knew there would come a time to use the money he'd been stashing, but right now there simply wasn't anything interesting to spend it on.

"Probably."

"Mind if I join the search? Something about her intrigues me and I want to be sure I'm not fantasizing about some twelve-year-old kid." Mitch shuddered and Phoenix had worried about the same thing—more than once. There was a sophistication in her communication he felt could only come from age and education, but that didn't mean they might not be chatting up some fifty-year-old man who only left his house to breeze through the local fast food drive-thru. *Another terrifying prospect.*

"No, I don't mind. Hell, I'd appreciate the help. I'm tired of having my ass handed to me every time I try to track her down. I've shown Micah some of the smoke screens she's thrown my way and he wants to hire her." They both laughed because anyone who could elude Phoenix was damned good. He'd built in a number of ways to track games because there was always the chance a participant would use their online persona for something nefarious. Phoenix wanted to be prepared to help law enforcement should that happen, but Athena was living up to her name.

Phoenix was glad his friend was showing an interest in the mysterious Athena, from what he'd heard, Mitch hadn't played much in the past year or two. Evidently he'd been interested in a former Air Force captain, but she'd moved on leaving Mitch reeling from a break up he hadn't seen coming.

"What's your cover for the press conference?" Mitch's question didn't surprise him. They'd been friends long enough for Mitch to know Phoenix showing up in Texas two days before the press conference wasn't a coincidence.

"Well, I'm Ms. Rodrick's new media contact for puttin' a stop to Joelle's nonsense, darlin'. After all, how dare a trouble-makin' lil nobody like Joelle Phillips interfere with the ambitions of a woman as important as Ms. Rodrick." Phoenix knew his southern accent wasn't perfect, but the look on Mitch's face was something between shock and horror.

"She'll make you in a New York minute. Hell, most third graders wouldn't be fooled by that shit." Swiping his hand through his hair, Mitch shook his head. "I'll talk to the team, but in the meantime, send me everything you've got. I want to read all the conversations between you two. And for God's sake, let's have some fun with those sweet little subs who think they've gotten off so easy."

CORAL WAS SO close to her goal she was sure she'd dodged another bullet. She'd carried the last tray of drinks almost the entire length of the pool without the plug in her ass doing anything but annoying her. All she had to do was make it another ten feet as she'd be able to set the tray of snacks down on the glass table where Sage sat waiting. *Don't tempt fate, Coral Anne, it always comes back to bite you in the ass.*

Looking up, she saw Sage sitting casually beside the table watching her intently. His laser-like focus zeroed in on her breasts as they bounced beneath the last narrow strip of PVC tape covering them. *The one that didn't even reach the outer edges of her areolas? That piece of tape? Does that even count?* She'd known it was too much to hope he'd bind her boobs with enough of that damned tape. No, he'd folded the four-inch wide tape over so the two-inch wide strip did almost nothing to hide her nipples even if she stood perfectly still. But since all of his shenanigans during their honeymoon had erased what little modesty she'd had to begin with, she tried to not focus on the fact men she barely knew were seeing far too much.

Remembering how he'd pulled her onto his lap at one of the dance clubs they'd gone to sent a hot rush to her sex. How he'd managed to free his impressive cock without anyone around them noticing was a mystery, but no one missed her moans of pleasure as he'd rocked her back and forth in time with the music. Of course, anyone who'd been trying to politely pretend they weren't watching had abandoned their attempts when her new husband pinched her throbbing clit sending her over the edge of a screaming release. She'd fallen over before she'd been able to think about how much attention her orgasm was going to get. Finding out later he'd carefully selected who would be nearby hadn't done much to dim her embarrassment.

She was only five foot away and closing in on the table when the thin membrane with all those tiny wires circling her clit roared to life. Cripes, she'd been a shivering bundle of need by the time Sage managed to get the devilish device in place, but now the demon-possessed device was going to steal her sanity. Coral froze in place unable to take another step. Her mind was scrambling to pull all the things happening around her into alignment as the pulses of rapture bubbled closer and closer to the surface. The membrane felt exactly like Sage's fingers, the only reason she knew he wasn't the one drawing slow circles around her clit was because he was sitting a few feet away smiling like a cat getting ready to pounce on a canary. Even without the electronic device vibrating against her clit, his lust-filled look would have had her sinking quickly into a bottomless pit of need.

Looking down, Coral realized her hands were empty. *What happened to the tray?* A disembodied voice to her right whispered, "Don't worry about the tray, sweet girl." Coral recognized the voice. Her last few functioning brain cells knew Master Nate was a friend of Sage's, but he certainly hadn't shown her any mercy earlier. She'd gotten the same swats Joelle had been given, but she'd been grateful he hadn't cut away the thin PVC covering her ass. Her new husband had vowed to put some weight on her during their month long honeymoon and damned if he hadn't succeeded. Those extra few pounds seemed to please him, but she was certainly less than thrilled.

Somewhere in the back of her mind, Coral's insecurities struck a match coming to life with a deafening roar. It shocked her to realize the overwhelming need pounding in her sex was being overshadowed by her fear of failing her new husband. The reality was, the other submissives participating in tonight's fun were all experienced in the lifestyle she'd only recently been introduced to. God, just thinking about all the ways she could screw this up was intensely humbling.

Focusing her attention on Sage, everything else faded into the background. Zeroing in on the man she planned to spend the rest of her life with helped her clear the static out of her mind. She was drawn to him like a magnet to steel, their attraction so strong it made her knees weak. She was grateful he hadn't risen from his seat. He was giving her time to work it out. *If he believes in you, you owe it to him to believe in yourself.* Her small epiphany was enough to let her take the first step. His answering smile and nod of approval sent her racing into his arms.

Sage battled with himself to stay seated as his beautiful bride fought an internal battle he knew would decide their future in the lifestyle. Being a Dominant was a big part of who he was, but his love for the woman standing so close, yet so far, was exponentially greater. He'd almost gone to her, but Phoenix's voice came through the small ear bud loud and clear. "Let her do it. She won't ever forgive herself if you have to rescue her. Save the knight in shining armor for something big...and you know it'll come soon enough. Those sisters of mine are going to get into plenty of trouble." Sage had to suppress his smile, because he agreed and they all knew what Joelle didn't, she was destined to be a Morgan, it was only a matter of time.

The communication devices were turning out to be a stroke of genius. Mitch picked up Joelle and Regi's conversation about swimming allowing Nate to make a well-timed change to their plan. He had to give his friend credit, he'd altered things so seamlessly neither of the women had suspected their private exchange had been anything but.

He wondered if Coral could hear Tobi's screams of frustration as her Doms tortured her by keeping her right on the precipice of release without letting her fall over the edge. He doubted she could hear anything over the din of her insecurities. Sage had worried he'd spend years mired in guilt over the hell his ex-girlfriend had put Coral through. Mackenzie's actions had been just shy of criminal or he'd have seen her locked in some dark hole in hell.

Coral hadn't done anything to deserve the bitch's wrath except catch his interest. The day they'd gotten married, he'd made a vow—one of the gifts he'd give her was the confidence she deserved. His greatest desire was for her to know how much she was loved.

JOELLE STOOD AGAINST the six-foot hedge watching as everyone held their collective breath. Coral had frozen mid-way between the wet bar and the table where Sage sat waiting for her. Joelle knew the devices her friend wore were only a part of her hesitance. Joelle remembered being the new girl at a play party. It was never easy being the least experienced submissive in the group, but the first party was almost unbearable. And, for a woman who already struggled with her self-esteem, it would easily be paralyzing.

Letting her gaze wander and as she'd suspected there were microphones hidden in every nook and cranny. Any conversation they'd thought was private had no doubt been monitored by whoever was manning the club's control center. Whoever was sitting in what she'd started thinking of as Spy Central was probably feeding information to the Doms through the small earbuds she'd noted they were wearing. That explained why Regi had been redirected around the pool.

Damn, she'd love to get a look inside the heart of the Prairie Winds Club. Earlier today they'd all been lounging by the pool when she'd said as much, causing both Tobi and Gracie to laugh at her. "We've never been allowed inside." Gracie had looked at Joelle with sympathy and understanding in her eyes.

In what Joelle was beginning to see was typical Tobi West style, the petite blonde whirlwind had stomped her foot in frustration. "It wasn't for a lack of trying. Damn, I got busted every damned time I tried to sneak in there. Hell's bells, it would have been easier to break into Fort fucking Knox."

"Listen to her, Joelle, she'd had enough spankings over this to be considered an expert." The sarcasm practically dripped from Gracie's words earning her a death glare from her spirited friend.

"You're a real comedian, Gracie. I recall you were on the spanking bench right beside me more than once." Returning her attention to Joelle, Tobi smiled ruefully. "Probably a good idea to erase that one from your bucket list. The *powers that be* tend to be totally anal on this particular point."

Gracie looked surprised. "Does this mean you're giving up your scheming to get inside their inner sanctum?" Gracie's dark eyes danced with mischief as she made no attempt to temper the hopeful tone of her voice.

"Dreamer." Tobi rolled her eyes at Gracie but her giggle brought a smile to Gracie's lips. "I'm just rethinking my strategy. There has to be a way to make it happen...I just haven't figured it out yet. Don't worry, I'll come up with a brilliant plan...eventually." Ordinarily a conversation like this would put Joelle off her desire to see or do something. She'd spent her entire life following rules, always playing the role of the quintessential good girl. *And look where it's gotten you.* Her harpy inner voice could be a relentless bitch sometimes, but in this case, she was right.

"Well, maybe someday I'll get the chance to see the control center in Mountain Mastery. Damn, maybe I'll build my own club somewhere, then no one can keep me out." She wasn't sure why it had seemed so important or why she was insanely focused on something that in the great scheme of things didn't matter at all. Shaking her head to clear out the wayward thoughts, Joelle looked around and smiled, wondering who was watching her watching them. Just thinking about sneaking into the control center at Mountain Mastery made her smile. Not only would it be fun to get one over on Master Nate, but the fact she was thinking about returning to Montana proved where her heart was. *Now I just have to make sure the men I've fallen for are thinking the same way.*

WE'RE WATCHING, JOELLE. Damn, I wish I could hear what's going through her mind because whatever it was, she'd just come to some kind of decision. Time to move, brother—you too, cousin. You need to present a united front. Phoenix's words spoken directly into his ear was all the encouragement Brandt needed. Ryan's nod let him know his cousin was in agreement. They'd waited long enough. Stepping forward in a move so well coordinated it looked choreographed, he and Ryan brought themselves to their full height. The move snapped Joelle from her thoughts, her eyes widened as the sweet flush of arousal washed over her chest. *Perfect.* Crooking his finger, he beaconed her closer and was beyond pleased when she didn't hesitate to move to them.

"We've been waiting all evening for a chance to be alone with you, minx." Brandt deliberately pitched his voice low, he wanted her to hear how much he wanted her.

"We've got an important question for you. But first, we've got a scene planned. Let's move inside." Joelle nodded even as her eyes darkened and took on the unmistakable glassy look of a sub getting into the perfect headspace. At her nod, they led her into the club's large main room. Stepping up on the center stage, Ryan saw Joelle's eye flick to the large ring behind him, but she quickly brought her eyes back to his. "Do you trust us, baby?"

"Yes, Sir. Completely." Her response had been immediate and spoken without hesitation letting him know she was ready for what they had planned. Securing her arms and legs inside the large frame before attaching the restraint circling her waist, Brandt watched the goose bumps race over her skin each time he caressed her smooth skin with the rough pads of his fingers. Standing in front of her, Brandt framed her face between his hands. Slanting his lips over hers, he didn't bother with preliminaries—this was all about possession and staking a claim no one would misinterpret. The scene they'd planned would take her over the edge quickly, they'd learned exactly how to send their woman into orbit. But the real goal was to help clear her mind. They didn't want her thinking to be cluttered by desire when they asked her to wear their collar. The diamond choker felt heavy in his pocket, it wasn't the weight of the lovely piece of jewelry they'd chose—it was its significance that kept him hyper-aware of it tucked against his leg in its slim velvet case.

Stepping back, Brandt was satisfied with the dazed look in her eyes—it was nice to know he wasn't the only one affected by the kiss they'd shared. Ryan leaned over her shoulder letting the silk scarf in his hand flutter softly over her breasts. Watching her nipples draw up into tight berries was too much to resist. While Ryan tied the black silk over her eyes, Brandt pulled first one tight bud and then the other into his mouth, sucking until he felt her body begin to tremble against the press of his lips. Brandt knew he could send her over the edge in seconds, but he wanted her desperate for what they could give her. *I want your heart and your head, love. I won't settle for anything else and neither will Ry.*

"OH NO, MINX. Not yet. We've only just started. We're going to make this night one you'll remember for the rest of your life," Brandt's words were whispered against the slope of her shoulder between soft kisses and stinging nips. When she shifted in an effort to get closer to him, she realized two things. First, shifting wasn't an option because she was bound securely. And second, her contracting muscles had noted the missing plug. *When did they remove it?*

"I see you've noticed the plug is gone, baby. Not to worry, we're planning to replace it with something much more interesting soon enough." Ryan's words now came from in front of her and were accompanied by the teasing sensation of leather strips dancing over the top slopes of her breasts. "Tell me how it feels, baby. I want to know exactly where your head is every step of the way tonight." Oh geez, she could already feel herself sliding into that magical place where her only thoughts were about chasing the pleasure, and he wanted a running monologue about how she felt?

"If you don't give him what he wants, he'll stop, minx. Contrary to what everybody thinks, I'm not the bad ass and he's not the charmer." Oh, she'd figured that out all on her own. The two of them swapped personas like hormonal teenagers...it was spooky how quickly they could switch roles.

Deciding honesty was the best choice, Joelle blurted out the words before she went under for the third time. "I'm already drowning in pleasure. I know you've only started, but I think it speaks volumes that I was so lost in the kiss I didn't even realize you'd removed the plug." Ryan continued to flick the soft strands of the flogger in a deliberately erratic pattern over her chest, keeping her unsure where the next bite would be. The leather strips were lighting up the nerve endings on the surface of her skin making it feel like little fairies in cleats were tap dancing everywhere the flogger struck. When he moved to her back, Joelle lost her ability to speak for several long minutes. Ryan tied the silk scarf over her eyes and without that distraction, she could lose herself in the moment. She let the increasing intensity of the flogger take her further into the quiet space in her head where nothing mattered but their touch.

"Do you know what we want from you, love?" Ryan's words were a warm rush of air moving against the shell of her ear. The air around her was almost vibrating with energy, but she didn't feel the leather slap of the flogger. *When did he stop?*

"Minx, your other Master asked you a question." Brandt's words had come from in front of her, but she couldn't remember being asked a question. "Ry, I think you might have done your job too well, I'm not sure she's going to be able to answer any of our questions until she has a chance to vent some of the rampant sexual tension pouring out of every pore." *Yes! What he said! Venting would be good...as long as it means I get to come.*

Chapter Eighteen

Two Days Later…

WAITING FOR THE press conference to start was excruciating. Joelle ran the tips of her fingers over the diamond choker resting at the base of her throat surprised at the *settled* feeling its weight brought her. The collaring ceremony Ryan and Brandt had surprised her with two nights ago would always be one of her most precious memories. She'd learned later they'd turned down Tobi and Gracie's offers of help, choosing instead to plan everything themselves. They'd even ordered flowers and selected food for a small reception after the intimate ceremony. The sheer robe they'd given her after she'd knelt in front of them to receive her collar hadn't offered much in the way of coverage, but knowing it was something they'd chosen for her warmed her heart. And now, every time one of her men noticed her touching the pretty line of diamonds their eyes softened, their emotions written so clearly in their expressions.

The scene at the Prairie Winds Club had connected the three of them in ways Joelle hadn't known possible. She had a feeling the connection was going to be important in the coming weeks because there wasn't any doubt there was a storm brewing on the horizon. The leaked video might have had set the stage, but today all the major networks were on hand and she knew they'd be relentless. But thanks to Tobi's wisdom, the dress rehearsal she'd had a few days ago had given her confidence a big boost. Even though she was nervous, she was also prepared.

The tall women wearing press credentials and leaning casually against the wall near the door caught Joelle's attention because the other reporters were all waiting in the medical center's enormous conference room. Leaning close to Brandt and nodding toward the reporter, Joelle asked, "Why isn't she waiting in with the others?" Even though he was standing with his back to the door, he didn't turn around to see who she'd asked about. He smiled knowingly down at her without answering. "I know reporters need to be alert to their surroundings, but she appears to be hyper-aware despite the casual pose.

Brandt still hadn't responded, but his raised brow told her he was more than a little surprised by her observation. "And those shoes are really hideous. What was the word Jen used the other day? Oh, yes, they're *fugly*. Evidently Jen is some sort of word blending phenomenon." This time, several of the men in the room coughed at the same time, the hands over their mouths failing to hide their guilty smiles. Joelle narrowed knowing eyes at Brandt.

To her credit, the woman in question didn't react, she casually pulled her phone from her jacket pocket and studied it as if it were the most interesting thing in the world. *And look at her hands. Those aren't the hands of a professional woman. They're too large and much too meaty. Hmmm*

Deciding to test her theory that everyone in the room could hear her, including the man dressed as a woman beside the door, Joelle smiled to herself. "I have to go to the rest room. I saw it on the way in. I'll be right back."

Stepping away from Brandt before he could grab her, she wanted to laugh because every man in the room went on point immediately. *Yes, boys and girls, the audio-visual show has begun. When the car begins to move, make sure you keep your hands and feet inside at all time. Now, sit back and enjoy the show.*

Even the faux reporter was suddenly fidgeting. *Not looking forward to shadowing me into the ladies room? Well, honey, it sucks to be you. I want to know what the hell is going on.* As expected, the reported entered the restroom's lavishly decorated anteroom less than a minute later. Joelle was ready and waiting, but before she'd uttered a word the door opened again and she found herself face to face with Helen Rodrick.

As strange as it seemed, it was the man pretending to be a female reporter moving alongside the hateful woman glaring at her that steeled Joelle's resolve. As a candidate for the presidency, the woman had a Secret Service detail and the fact she'd slipped past them told Joelle a lot about how the woman glaring at her planned for this little meet and greet to go down.

"You just don't get it, do you?" Helen Rodrick's voice oozed pure venom.

"Evidently not, Ms. Roderick. Perhaps you'd like to enlighten me before your security detail catches up with you. And I'm sure the reporter standing beside you would be interested in knowing why it's so important for you to keep this breakthrough quiet." Joelle hoped she hadn't misread the reporter's reason for positioning himself closer to the old hag. Damn, why on Earth was she so focused on preventing Joelle from sharing what she'd discovered. The only possible explanation was the former senator cared more about money than people…and that baffled Joelle.

She was actually grateful for the opportunity to confront the woman who'd caused her to question herself. Joelle was embarrassed she'd let fear keep her from doing what she should have done in the very beginning. The only saving grace in the whole mess was she'd found Brandt and Ryan. "Why couldn't you just keep your information on your computer or stashed in your apartment like a *normal* person? Christ, woman, you've been a pain in my ass."

"Are you the one who broke into my apartment?" Joelle knew her voice reflected how utterly appalled she was by the depth of the woman's unethical behavior.

"Don't be ridiculous, I didn't go myself. The last place I'd want to be seen would be coming out of your building the same evening as a break in." Her face contorted as if she'd smelled something dead as she continued, "Hell, I wouldn't want to be seen in that building...well, ever. Really, I don't think you could have found a less interesting place to live if you'd tried. You've obviously spent way too much time in your precious lab, dear. Your lack of class must be a horrible embarrassment to your father." Joelle felt as if someone had yanked the rug out from under her feet. Damn if the woman hadn't zeroed in on one of her biggest insecurities.

"I don't really have the time or desire to chat with you about my relationship with my father. Just tell me why you're here because I have a press conference to get to." Joelle felt her control slipping and it was just a matter of time before someone noticed she'd been gone too long.

Helen must have seen Joelle's glance toward the reporter because she followed her gaze before resettling her attention on Joelle. "Don't worry about him. We've been working together for weeks. He's going to tell the world about how you attacked me when I tried to leave." She pulled a large knife from her purse and everything about her posture seemed to shift right before Joelle's eyes. Helen might not have noticed, the subtle shift in the reporter's stance, but Joelle didn't miss it.

The woman's lunge was so quick and so unexpected Joelle didn't have time to do anything but gasp in surprise as the knife pierced her side. The white-hot pain dropped her to her knees and it took her several seconds to realize the screaming in her ears was her own voice bouncing around the small space. Had the reporter not shoved her attacker at the last moment the knife would have been buried to the hilt directly into Joelle's heart. Realizing how close she'd come to losing her life was frightening, but those thoughts were quickly eclipsed by the pandemonium erupting around her. Despite all the shouts from the people pouring into the small room, Joelle felt like she was drifting further and further away from the noise as the darkness at the edges of her vision closed in. *Why are they all yelling? It's just a small cut. I'll be fine if everyone would just calm down. Maybe I'll just rest my eyes for a few minutes while they sort it out.*

RYAN HIT THE door at a full run slamming it into the wall sending chunks of sheetrock falling in his wake. He was at Joelle's side and knew within seconds how life threatening her injury was. He'd seen several soldiers die from bullet wounds to the exact location of the knife wound she'd suffered. He also knew if she'd sustained this injury anywhere but a trauma level medical facility, they wouldn't have a prayer of saving her. Thankfully, he'd completed his residency in this hospital so he knew exactly where he needed to take her. Peeling off his shirt, he pressed it against the wound and lifted her gently into his arms. Running down the hall, Ryan directed Brandt letting his cousin clear the path and shove open the doors to the outer surgical suite. Two of the men Brandt pushed out the way were surgeons Ryan recognized. At his shout for help, they didn't hesitate to follow Ryan into the first empty prep-room he found.

Ryan pushed Brandt out of the room as the surgeons set to work. He knew he'd see the haunted look on his cousin's face in his nightmares for years to come. Brandt's last mission had ended horribly and the aftermath of seeing most of his team wiped out had sent the team leader into an emotional spiral. It had taken months for Brandt to begin living again and it was easy to see him sliding into the abyss of fear. "We won't lose her. I swear to you I won't let her go. But you've got to let us do our jobs. Go get the bitch who did this."

Brandt's eyes lit with fire and Ryan was relieved to see him channel his fear into a purpose-filled expression. He nodded and turned to go, but stopped to grab Ryan's arm. "She's our world. Take good care of her." Ryan fought back the emotion as he nodded before they turned back to their respective tasks. There wasn't a doubt in his mind the rest of the team had already taken Helen Rodrick into custody, but he also knew they'd be waiting for Brandt before they turned her over to the local authorities. *Take the bitch apart, cuz.*

SITTING BESIDE JOELLE'S bed watching the gentle rise and fall of her chest was the only thing keeping Brandt from going out of his mind. His guilt felt like an elephant sitting on his chest. He'd been so focused on getting as much on tape as possible to ensure Helen Rodrick's conviction, he'd held the team back too long. Threading his fingers with hers, Brandt let the soft beeping of her heart monitor push back the darkness threatening to overtake him again. He'd been so lost in his thoughts he hadn't heard the door open, but he'd known immediately the large hand resting on his shoulder belonged to his dad.

"I can almost feel the guilt pouring off you, son. And damned if I don't understand exactly what you're going through. I've kicked myself a thousand times for not taking the initiative to help you when you first moved home. You proved yourself capable of fighting your way out of the pit you'd fallen into, but damn it—you shouldn't have had to do it alone. I'll always feel like I let you down. But son, I'm telling you right now—I'm not going to stand back and watch you slide down that slippery slope again." His dad pulled a chair close and when he'd settled, his eyes met Brandt's. For the first time in his life, Brandt saw vulnerability in his father's eyes, and it shocked him to realize the man he'd considered a tower of strength thought he'd failed to help one of his sons. When he started to speak, his dad shook his head. "No, it's true. Morgans don't let one another down and I was so focused on getting your brother set up in his new role I let you flounder. Hell, I even managed to convince myself I was doing you a favor by letting you work through it yourself."

His dad swiped his hand over his face in frustration. "Well, it's in the past, I can't change it but I can damned well make sure I don't make the same mistake again. I'm telling you right now, I might be older than I was when you were a kid, but I'm still your father. And I'm not going to sit idly by and watch you tear yourself up over this. That gorgeous woman deserves all of you, not just the guilt-ridden bits you'll have left to share until you pull yourself through it again."

"Dad." Brandt's voice was pitched low and sounded ominous even to him, but his dad shook his head.

"I'm not backing down on this, son. You need us and we're here for you. But you need to pull yourself together because Joelle is a brilliant young woman who isn't going to want your guilt or pity. You think about *that*, boy. Cherish the gift you've been given, because I promise you there is nothing like the love of a good woman to make your life worth living." His dad didn't give him a chance to argue, he just made his way quietly out of the room.

Ryan slipped in as his dad stepped out. Moving to the other side of Joelle's bed, he brushed the back his fingers down Joelle's pale cheek. "She'd going to be fine, you know. The damage wasn't as bad as I'd originally thought, but we're still damned lucky we were here. Don't beat yourself up, hell, Mitch was standing a few feet away and didn't have time to stop her. For an old broad, Helen Rodrick is damned quick with a knife."

"Mitch? Is that the reporter's name?" They both looked down at Joelle, her eyes alight with mischief. "I wondered. It took me a few minutes, but I'd figured out she wasn't really a woman. I'm grateful you'd thought ahead and he was close by. He saved my life and if you hadn't put him in place who knows what might have happened." Brant felt the guilt he'd been fighting burn off like a morning fog, and his heart filled to the point of bursting.

Ryan grinned as he looked at Joelle. "You're amazing, baby. And don't think for a minute we're letting you out of our sight again. Just so you know, I went toe-to-toe with the head surgical nurse over your collar. She wasn't at all pleased I wouldn't tell her how to unlock it." Brandt laughed because he'd heard a couple of nurses discussing the battle of wills they'd watched take place outside the operating room. Ryan had won the war, but he'd gotten a few verbal battle scars in the process—the older nurse hadn't gone down without a fight.

Brandt leaned over to press a kiss against Joelle's forehead. "You own my heart, minx. I know we should wait and give you the romantic setting you deserve for this—but the truth is I don't want to wait."

"I agree. This way she can pick out her own ring. Marry us, baby."

"Jesus, Ry—that wasn't a proposal, it was a command." Brandt looked at his cousin and shook his head.

Ryan shrugged off the criticism. "Of course, it was a command. If we *ask,* she might say no. I didn't want to take a chance."

Looking down, Brandt saw tears pooling in Joelle's soft gray eyes. "Love, I hope those are happy tears because we aren't going to take no for an answer."

"I know it wasn't a question, but I still want a chance to say *yes.* But don't think you're off the hook for the hearts and flowers proposal. As soon as my fiancé—the doctor—springs me, we're going shopping. I'm really looking forward to finding something worthy of the two best men a woman could ever dream of finding." *From your lips to God's ears, minx. We'll do our best to make your every dream come true.*

Chapter Nineteen

Three months later...

JOELLE STUFFED A handful of cash through the window of the taxi before dashing into the airport terminal. She'd barely gotten through the revolving door when a security guard stepped into her path. "Are you Joelle Phillips?" She nodded and his harsh expression immediately softened, a small smile curving the corners of his mouth. "Come with me, please." She had no clue what she'd done to be in trouble, but she also knew better than to argue. When she hesitated to get into the golf cart, he looked at her with a raised brow. She recognized the look and even though she might not know why he was whisking her across the terminal, she damned well recognized a Dom when she met one. He simply nodded, "Good girl. They told me you'd know."

Oh, she knew all right. She'd been living with first one Dom and then another for the past four months. Brandt and Ryan had been traveling back and forth between Washington, D.C. and Montana while she'd struggled to wrap up the endless string of hearings associated with her discovery and Helen Rodrick's indictment. Joelle knew the woman would never spend a day behind bars, but her political career was in shambles. Knowing the woman would never hold political office again was enough for

Joelle, but her men didn't seem to agree. The Morgans were calling in a lot of favors to ensure the woman paid for targeting Joelle.

What was supposed to be a six-week hearing had stretched into three months when Joelle's father died suddenly before he could testify before the Senate committee investigating the Phillips Pharmaceutical's board of directors. The sell-off of stock had set off similar runs in other drug companies. It had taken Joelle weeks to find out who'd been buying up the stock, but all roads finally led to her future fathers-in-law. Between the stock she'd already held and the shares she'd gotten after her father's death, Joelle held thirty percent. But with Dean and Don Morgan's twenty-two shares, they now held majority-voting interest, something that pleased her very much.

Today was the first board meeting since the shift in power. She'd enjoyed being the one to introduce the board's newest members even if they hadn't been in the room. They'd participated via a video link and hadn't hesitated to share their vision for the company's future. Any board member who didn't share their vision was given the opportunity to sell their shares. It had taken every ounce of self-control she'd been able to scrape together to keep from laughing at the mortified expressions when Dean had stated their terms. Damn, she'd wished Dean and Don had been able to personally attend the meeting. They'd both sworn they had something more important scheduled, but for some reason, she'd gotten the impression she was being bamboozled.

When the golf cart she was riding in passed through the gate for private arrivals and departures Joelle cast a questioning look at her driver. He grinned and pointed to the large white jet with Morgan Holdings emblazoned on the side. Shaking her head, Joelle's heart swelled with joy. She was marrying Brandt and Ryan the day after tomorrow and evidently they hadn't wanted to risk her missing her flight. Climbing on board, she was surprised to see both Dean and Don standing beside an intricately carved wooden bar. Dean was the first to see her, setting his drink down he stepped toward her and grinned.

"As you can see, we had something far more important to take care of."

Don moved to his brother's side, hands shoved deep in his pockets and rocked up on his heels grinning. He looked like an older version of Ryan and in that moment she knew she'd just seen a glimpse of her future. "It's true. Neither of us has a daughter and we didn't want to take a chance on you changing your mind. After all, you asked us to walk you down the aisle."

"And we're looking forward to that honor. So we wanted to make sure you arrived in Montana safely." Their impish smiles were more than she could resist. She hugged them both before looking around appreciatively the aircraft's luxurious interior. Dean laughed. "It was part of the incentive package to keep Sage on board as CEO when we merged. Now that I'm going to be a grandfather, there will need to be some more changes made to our original plan, but this will make the commute a lot easier." *Oh, indeed it will. Holy shit, this isn't your average commuter's idea of a ride to work.*

"We'll let the boys tell you all about what's been happening while you're lying on the beach soaking up the sun." Don's grin told Joelle he knew exactly where they were going on their honeymoon and she'd be willing to bet her Phillips stock it wasn't anywhere near a beach. Ryan and Brandt had refused to tell her their destination. She'd been told she only needed to bring her purse, that they had everything else covered. Personally, Joelle would have preferred to find a nearby flat surface and sleep for a week. The past four months had been positively grueling. Hell, she hadn't even been able to plan her own wedding. Thankfully, her future mothers-in-law had been thrilled to step in. Coral had been charged with making sure they didn't get too carried away, something that had, according to her friend, taken a Herculean effort.

Knowing her best friend was also going to be her sister-in-law was enough to make Joelle jump up and down for joy. She was getting two amazing husbands and the large, loving family she'd always dreamed of. Brandt and Ryan had been sending her pictures of the lab Morgan Holdings was building but they'd refused to send her any pictures of the home they were scrambling to finish.

Dean's voice brought her back to the present. "You know, she doesn't look as happy as I'd hoped she'd be. I wonder if we showed her the pictures we took of the house if they'd earn us any extra points?"

Oh, they had her attention now. Joelle bounced on the balls of her feet as the fatigue she'd been feeling morphed into excitement. Settling between them, she fastened her seat belt when they began taxiing down the runway. They passed her picture after picture sharing in her happiness in a way her father never would have been able to do. And while she missed him, she wasn't going to waste a moment of her time languishing in sadness while she was with her future dads. She'd grieved and vowed not to let anything in her past hold her back. She'd done a lot to help others live the long, happy lives they deserved, and now it was time for her to enjoy the best of what life had to offer as well.

Don Morgan brushed a tear from her cheek. "What's

the matter, sweetheart? Feeling a little overwhelmed?" *How did he know?*

"You know, for a couple of guys who didn't have any daughters, you're really acing this dad thing."

"Damn, darlin', I think that's one of the nicest compliments I've ever gotten. And I'm sure it's one of the nicest things a woman's ever said to my brother because frankly he's just not as nice as I am."

Dean looked at his brother and rolled his eyes. "Don't listen to him. You'll find out soon enough, I'm going to be the better father-in-law. Hell, everybody knows this except my kid brother."

Joelle couldn't hold back her laughter. Suddenly, every hurdle she had to maneuver to get to this moment faded into the background. She was finally on her way *home* to the men who hadn't taken no for an answer.

Epilogue

COLT MORGAN PULLED into the alley behind O'Donnell Hardware, parking his large truck beneath the carport behind the store. He hadn't seen any lights in the small apartment, but somebody evidently had or he wouldn't have been called out at this ungodly hour. Fuck, he'd only been in bed an hour when Brandt's deputy called saying he'd had a report of a light on in the unoccupied apartment. He loved his hometown, but there were times having everyone up in your business was enough to make him want to pull his hair out.

His new sister-in-law had lived in the small apartment above the store before marrying Colt's oldest brother, Sage. Of course, his damned brother had taken Coral on a cruise to celebrate their four and a quarter month anniversary, or some such shit, so he wasn't available to go on this particular wild goose chase. Sage bought the store when Charlotte O'Donnell decided traveling sounded more appealing than another Montana winter—*wise woman*. Coral spent a lot of time at the store where she'd worked, making a lot of improvements while keeping the charm of a building who'd served the people of their sleepy mountain town for almost a hundred years.

He might be exhausted, but Colt was also relieved the last of this season's hay crop had been cut, baled, and safely stored around the ranch well ahead of the coming winter.

Other ranches routinely did another cutting late in the season, but the Morgan Ranch left that growth in place hoping to catch more snow. The extra snow meant precious moisture for next year's crop. He'd fallen into bed relieved to finally be looking at a full eight hours of sleep before trying to catch up with the outside world. He hadn't seen a television for more than a week—hell, World War III could have broken out for all he knew. *Fuck! I should have shut my damned phone off.*

Moving the large clay pot at the base of the stairs, Colt picked up one of the spare keys he knew was hidden there and started up the stairs. Swearing to himself as one of the steps moved under his foot, Colt vowed to stop by later and secure the loose step—he didn't want to take a chance Coral might slip and fall. Even though no one was currently living in the small apartment, they had been making improvements hoping to have it ready to rent soon and she made the trip up the outdoor staircase several times each day.

Sage was interviewing managers for the store even though his pregnant wife didn't know what her husband was planning. He'd tried to warn his brother that excluding his new bride from such an important decision was a whole new level of stupid, but Sage had never been big on taking advice from his younger brothers. Colt laughed to himself, his big brother was fixin' to be taken down a peg or two by his sweet wife and his younger brothers were all looking forward to the show.

When the door opened without the key, Colt swore under his breath. Kip had been the last one working up here and Colt wondered where his head had been that he'd failed to secure the door. Fuck it, they were all wondering if the youngest Morgan brother was ever going to grow up and become a responsible adult. Slipping inside, Colt stifled a curse when he saw the door of the refrigerator was open. From the muffled ramblings and sound of the contents being moved around it was obvious someone was desperately looking for something to eat. *What the hell? What kind of burglar takes time to make himself a snack?* Stepping closer, he was about to yank the door further open to confront the refrigerator bandit when an unmistakable feminine voice made him freeze. Without moving so much as a muscle, he listened as she chattered softly to someone she thought had stolen her orange juice.

Leaning over he spotted familiar light blonde hair and had to hold back his chuckle at the brilliant streak of neon blue falling along the right side of her angelic face. Coral's friend Josie—known to the rest of the world as pop singing sensation Josephine Alta was frantically looking for a bottle of juice. Why the hell was a woman who made millions each year holed up in an unfinished apartment in Pine Creek, Montana?

She'd shown up for Sage and Coral's wedding—rocked his world and then vanished as quickly as she'd appeared. He'd followed her online as she'd done shows all over the country during a tour so successful they'd been adding dates in every city. Stepping silently behind her, Colt simply waited patiently for her to find the bottle of orange juice she was frantically looking for.

"HEY, REFRIGERATOR FAIRY, where did you hide the damned orange juice? I know I left one of those little bottles in here. Don't tell me you shared with your sprite buddies because that's just gonna suck. Damn it, nobody asked me if they could drink the last bottle. Coral warned me this place was under construction but she didn't say anything about it being overrun with juice steeling wee folk." Josie leaned her forehead against the fridge and groaned. *That's it. I've officially lost my mind. I should have known I'd tip over the edge if I didn't learn to say no. Damn it, where is that freaking juice?*

"Come on, come on. I know it's in here. I can't go to the damned store…somebody will recognize me and splash my damned picture all over the internet, then he'll find me again. Coral will be home in a few days and then she can help me figure out what to do. Fucking hell, I need that juice. If I don't have it, I won't be able to sleep. And, I really need to sleep." And wasn't that the understatement of the decade. Damn, she hadn't had a good night's sleep in weeks. The notes left in her dressing rooms around the country had been frightening enough to keep her awake at night, but returning to her home in LA to find it gutted had been terrifying. *Who steals everything and then tears out entire walls, for heaven's sake?*

Sagging in defeat, Josie was losing the battle to hold back the hot tears of frustration burning at the back of her eyes. Everything had spiraled out of control during the last few weeks. Her final shows seemed more like a slow slide into some b-rated horror movie than the end of a hugely successful music tour. She'd lost so much weight her wardrobe assistant had been forced to rework every one of her stage outfits, but she'd been too unsettled to eat. *Damn, I really wanted that juice.*

She was exhausted, hungry, and scared. Josie surrendered to the tears as she stood and leaned her forehead against the closed door of the refrigerator trying again to regain her composure. "Fucking hell. All I wanted was some sleep and a bottle of fucking orange juice." Her voice caught on a sob of frustration, that quickly morphed into a scream when she heard the distinctive scape of a shoe across the floor behind her.

Spinning around, hands raised in defense, Josie screamed. The part of her brain that recognized the man moving toward her was shoved aside by the larger part drowning in blind terror. She felt strong hands wrap around her upper arms stilling her attempts to escape. "Stop. Josie, sweetheart, it's Colt." Something in the commanding tone of his voice finally cut through the fear and she sagged against him. *Safe.* The word was playing a continuous loop in her head as the need for the warmth of human connection had her climbing up his toned body like a spider monkey.

His arms banded around her, pressing her against his chest. The fear she'd been fighting for weeks, compounded with the surge of adrenaline she'd gotten a few seconds ago, drained the last of her strength. In the safety of his embrace, Josie finally let go.

COLT HAD NEVER felt so blinded by rage as he had when he'd seen the look in Josie's eyes. The expression had been something between haunted and terrorized. He'd never seen that expression in anyone's eyes—fuck, the look would haunt him for the rest of his life. Whoever was responsible was living on borrowed time.

He moved into the small living room and settled on the overstuffed sofa. Huge gulping sobs wracked her too slender body as he stroked his hand up and down the length of her spine. *Jesus, Joseph, and sweet mother, Mary. How much weight has she lost?* He remembered thinking she was too thin the night they'd spent together, but she was positively *frail* now. Listening to her cry was going to tear his heart into small pieces. But he was going to let her get it all out before loading her up and taking her home. He'd heard the fear in her voice when she mentioned being found and she damned well wasn't safe here. *Christ, what's happened to her? I really need to watch the fucking news more.*

"I've got you, sweetheart. Let it all go. I'll never let anyone hurt you." *I'm not letting you run again either.*

THE END

Books by Avery Gale

The Wolf Pack Series

Mated – Book One
Fated Magic – Book Two
Tempted by Darkness – Book Three

Masters of the Prairie Winds Club

Out of the Storm
Saving Grace
Jen's Journey
Bound Treasure
Punishing for Pleasure
Accidental Trifecta
Missionary Position

The ShadowDance Club

Katarina's Return – Book One
Jenna's Submission – Book Two
Rissa's Recovery – Book Three
Trace & Tori – Book Four
Reborn as Bree – Book Five
Red Clouds Dancing – Book Six
Perfect Picture – Book Seven

Club Isola

Capturing Callie – Book One
Healing Holly – Book Two
Claiming Abby – Book Three

I would love to hear from you!

Email:

avery.gale@ymail.com

Website:

www.averygalebooks.com/index.html

Facebook:

facebook.com/avery.gale.3

Instagram:

avery.gale

Twitter:

@avery_gale